THE OTHER IN THE MIRROR

THE OTHER IN THE MIRROR

Edited by

Sehyr Mirza

YODAPRESS

YODA PRESS
79 Gulmohar Enclave
New Delhi 110 049
www.yodapress.co.in

ISBN 978-93-82579-79-3

Editors in charge: Ishita Gupta, Himadri Agarwal and Arpita Das
Typeset in Adobe Caslon Pro, 11/14.4
By MSourcing
Published by Arpita Das for YODA PRESS

Dedicated to my grandmother with love

‘It was the best of times, it was the worst of times, it was the age of wisdom, it was the age of foolishness, it was the epoch of belief, it was the epoch of incredulity, it was the season of light, it was the season of darkness, it was the spring of hope, it was the winter of despair.’

— Charles Dickens, A Tale of Two Cities

'Don't say that one lakh Hindus and one lakh Muslims died; say that two lakh human beings died. That two lakh human beings died is not such a great tragedy after all; the tragedy, in truth, is that those who killed and those who were killed, both have nothing to show for it.'

—Saadat Hassan Manto, short story Sahae

Contents

Preface

There are stories that you live. And there are stories that live with you. I've grown up with fragments of one such story—the most prized possession passed down to me by my grandmother. The story has been a guiding force through this anthology's journey. As a young girl growing up in Lahore, I always wanted to travel to my grandmother's birthplace, which happened to be on the other side of the border. I thought that my love and fascination to explore her roots would only remain a fantasy. Amidst the war hysteria and toxic nationalism prevalent in the hostile society we grew up in, it wasn't uncommon for this heartfelt desire to be trampled several times. My dream, however, seemed to be a step closer to reality when I finally got the visa and boarded the flight to India.

I noticed the bright sea-line mingling with the skies as I peeked out from the small airplane window on my way from Karachi to Bombay. Floating over the endless bends of the meandering blue waters, the thin and flat boats appeared like they had been cut from paper. The sea filled me with a deep sense of longing.

It seemed like the silence of the roaring tides was yearning to unleash the painful tales ensconced in the sea's bosom. Memories rippled through my mind as I lost myself in the depths of the waters. The stories narrated to me during the intimate hours spent with my grandmother started coming to life.

It was sometime in mid-August, 1947. My grandmother, Noor Jehan, then about sixteen years old, bid farewell to her homeland on a sea voyage from Bombay to Karachi.

The ship was cramped with a few thousand refugees—many who knew they might never return to their homeland. Their hissing sighs and prayers resonated in the air. They were voyaging, yet nobody awaited them. Their hearts grieved over what they had left behind, and what stood ahead was uncharted territory.

Fear clutched my grandmother's heart as she stood hand in hand with Vimla. The ship moved ahead, but her gaze remained fixed behind at the cityscape, gradually vanishing into the heavy black smoke spiralling out from the ship's funnel.

Flitting through the pages of my memories, I was reminded of the thick smoke clouds that'd glide across the room as I sat cross-legged in front of my grandmother, who'd gulp on her hookah hose while remembering her past. I would travel to Kota, Rajasthan, with her words.

My grandmother's family lived in a buzzing multicultural vicinity of the city. A vibrant central bazaar, now part of the old town of Kota, was lined with shops, hotels, local eateries, and some dwelling houses.

Passing through a maze of narrow alleys, she had collected her most adored pieces of jewellery, some sarees, some shawls, some silverware, some utensils, a tabletop mirror, and a bronze surma daani. Many of these objects, amid several photographs and letters, are stashed in one dedicated corner of my room. All these objects are living, breathing things that have their own character. These objects transport me to an unlived past, an unknown period, traversing me through unfamiliar places in the most enchanting of ways. They magically diminish the distance between the past and the present.

Listening to my grandmother, my mind would vividly visualize her memories. I'd often imagine her in a mint green saree. Adorned with jasmine flowers, her long black hair would be neatly braided down her back. Her expressive kohl-rimmed eyes would sparkle, as she'd race up the temple steps to ring the bells. She had a deep fascination for the rhythmic sounds of the temple bells—their dreamlike resonance still echoes in my mind along with her voice.

'It makes no difference if one prays at a temple, a mosque or a church – religions might have different names, but they all lead to the same path.'

Most of my grandmother's friends were Hindus. She would recall sailing down to the Jag Mandir stationed in the Kishore Sagar Lake. She would remember the barefoot strolls along the Chambal River with her friends. Reminiscing about the splendid celebrations of Diwali, she would often talk about lighting diyas and decorating her house along with Vimla.

Of all her friends, Vimla was the closest. She felt at home at my grandmother's residence. Having lost her own family at an early age, she considered my grandmother's parents as her own. She was a few years older than my grandmother. Both of them were soul sisters. They would sit for hours chatting up in the veranda of the house, or play the cat's cradle and spend the afternoons crocheting.

When the riots broke out in 1947, several Muslim families began moving to Pakistan. My grandmother's father had chosen to stay back in Kota until a ghastly night in the first week of August when a Muslim family in the Hindu-dominated neighbourhood of Kota was brutally attacked. One man's dead body was hung upside down at a chowk near the central bazaar. The fear among the Muslims began escalating into feelings of an alarming panic. My grandmother's family made the half-hearted eleventh-hour decision to flee to Pakistan.

My great grandfather was an artillery maker in the court of Maharao Bhim Singh II, the last ruling Maharaja of the princely state of Kota from 1940 to 1947. He turned to the prince's court to seek help. The prince made a futile attempt to persuade him to stay back, but the fear was such that my great-grandfather couldn't think otherwise.

'The sea route seems to be the safest. My guards will accompany you to the Port of Bombay, but from there onwards, you will be on your own,' he retorted.

Preparations had begun to flee to Pakistan. Only those objects from the house were packed that were important enough to keep the family safe and alive during the journey. Some other sentimental and precious belongings such as gold, jewellery, and some photographs were to be carried too.

It was far too risky to carry gold on a train journey amidst the ongoing chaos in the country. My great-grandfather, a seasoned craftsman and chemist, specialized in working with gold and other precious metals. He set about the gold melting and remolding process. The gold was melted and remolded into small round balls, wrapped in freshly kneaded flour dough. The gold was, thus, mixed in steel jars of gum berry fruit pickle, which the family clutched with them—as the last resort to begin life from scratch in a new country.

The day of departure finally arrived. The armed soldiers from the court of the Maharaja positioned themselves outside my grandmother's house. The Maharaja had commanded my grandmother's family to disguise themselves as Hindus during the train journey to Bombay. The women in the family replaced their dhoti-styled shararas and kurtas with sarees. My great grandmother and her daughter-in-law donned bindis and filled the parting of the hair with vermillion powder. The men passed the dhotis between their legs and tucked them at the back. Their white caps were replaced with red turbans, and tilak was applied to their foreheads.

Cold chills of panic swept through Vimla's heart. She held my grandmother's hand and took her to the temple they often visited together. The priest placed his hand on my grandmother's head to offer his blessings. 'The god is angry at the riots taking place in the city. Why else would the city be hit by such torrential thunderstorms?' he assured. My grandmother found herself in a quandary, yet she knew it was her last visit to the temple.

My great-grandfather's fear of leaving his duty, home, and his homeland in his mid-life was staring straight into his eyes. Those in the neighbourhood who remained untouched by hate had come to say the last goodbye to the family. A tumultuous storm of emotions was brewing within Vimla's heart.

My agonized great-grandfather locked the gate of his house and slipped the key into his waistcoat pocket. His throat tightened as unshed tears stung his eyes. He didn't have the courage to take one final look at his house but felt determined to return.

The caravan of ten people guarded by armed soldiers was set to leave for Bombay. Vimla came running behind. 'I always thought you'd change your mind about leaving,' she said as tears coursed down her cheeks. 'I know, you'll tell me that it is safe for me to stay here. But please, take me along,' she pleaded.

My great-grandfather gave in to her last appeal and was now responsible for ensuring the safety of his two daughters—a Hindu and a Muslim. The violence was at its peak, and the country had turned into a bloodbath by the second week of August. Men from the rival communities abducted and raped women to assert their masculine power. My great grandfather's voice cracked as he handed over two packets of poison to each of his daughters. 'If I am killed on our way to Bombay, you're both going to take this poison.'

Clinging tightly to one another on the train journey, Vimla and my grandmother terrifyingly witnessed the brutal incidents of the massacre, burnings and lootings. I'd see tears clouding my grandmother's eyes as she'd tell me how the warmth of Vimla's hand, firmly clasping hers, would constantly remind her that human relations are bigger than religions.

The twenty-five traumatic days spent at the camp in Karachi sucked all the hope from my great-grandfather's soul. People were dying of hunger and diseases in the camp. There were hardly any food provisions, and people ate and drank whatever they could find. My grandmother painfully witnessed her father growing weaker from depression and ailments.

She narrated to me an incident of Jinnah's visit to the camp when she rose from the crowd holding the dried scraps of meagre food offered to the migrants and screamed if this is what they deserved in the newly-created country, after all their sacrifices?

My great-grandfather would often blankly stare at his house key and burst into tears. He didn't live long enough to be able to open the doors of his home again, which might not even exist now. My grandmother, too, could never get over the myth of returning to her birthplace.

She lived for thirty years in Abadan, Iran, and twenty-five years in Lahore, but her soul resided in the streets of Kota. She would tell me about the cargo ships voyaging from India to the coastal town of Abadan, which turned into makeshift bazaars on Sundays. Whenever my grandmother would visit these, she inquired if they had something from Kota? She would eagerly collect items that reminded her of her beloved city.

Seated in her bedroom in the winters of the late 1990s, I remember her smile when she'd tell me that Vimla was coming to see her. Vimla had settled down in Rawalpindi with her husband and three sons. They would both chat for hours whenever she visited Lahore, recalling the happy memories from Kota.

At an early age, I witnessed the Partition—the pain, anger, sorrow, and anguishof it—through my grandmother's eyes that remained unclouded by hate. I believe that she had inadvertently passed on her intense sense of nostalgia to me. I never get tired of digging into the old trunks of my memories. I often relive her stories, and my inquisitiveness and passion churn out of these.

On my return from a sentimental visit to Rajasthan, I was determined to put together an anthology as a culmination of my love for my grandmother. Her art of storytelling had shaped my life. I wanted to explore storytelling as a creative process to fashion lived experiences into fictional narratives to touch the hearts of readers. I wanted to collect twenty stories from India and Pakistan that gave a more significant meaning to the notions of compassion, kindness, tolerance, co-existence and non-violence.

My grandmother would say that the chaotic and catastrophic sequence of events that emerged during Partition had only two sides. One was the side of kindness, non-violence and compassion. And the other, the side of cruelty, violence and hate. Which side we choose is the question she left me with.

Acknowledgements

I would like to express my sincere gratitude to all the authors who contributed to this anthology and believed in the significance of this project, which is truly a first of its kind literary collaboration between Pakistan and India. I would like to particularly thank Gulzar *saheb,* who has been an inspiration for the spirit behind this anthology from the very beginning.

My acknowledgements are due to Imran Khan, Adnan Rafiq and the United States Institute of Peace for all their support. Without their consistent camaraderie, this idea might not have seen the light of day. To Saadia Sabir and the team, many thanks for all your support.

Thank you is an understatement when it comes to Arpita Das, the superwoman behind Yoda Press, and her incredible team, for giving a lot of warmth to this book. I'd also like to especially thank the very-talented Priya Kuriyan for giving life to some of these characters in these stories with her remarkable illustration work. I want to thank all the translators for the brilliant translations of the Urdu and Hindi stories into English.

Many thanks to Rakhshanda Jalil, Manjri Sevak, Meenakshi Gopinath, Aryaman Bhatnagar, Vani Tripathi, Nina Sabnani, Shailja Chandara, Anil Jeenagar, Makarand Waingankar, Naeem Baig, Begum Rehana Undre, Aishee Meerza, Farideh Meerza, Amit Ranjan, Abdal Jafri, Kirti Raj Singh, Jameel Gulrays, Farah Zia, Beena Sarwar, Ish Madhu Talwar, Prem Chand Gandhi, Irshad Ameen, Vishwajyoti Ghosh and Rahul Roy, for being my strength, knowingly and unknowingly, at various stages of this book.

I would also like to extend my gratitude to the team of SAMAAJ, without which this project would perhaps have just remained an idea. Through their efforts, some stories from this anthology have been adapted into short animated films.

This book would not have been possible without the love and support of my family. Thank you is due to Ammar Aziz for his creative advice and endless support, and for pushing me to contribute one of my own stories to the anthology. Thank you to Nusrat Meerza and Maryam Saeed, for the hour-long reminiscences about my grandmother. Thank you to my father, Saeed Ahmed, for imbuing in me the love for fiction, literature, philosophy and activism and for all the intense literary and intellectual dialogues that have been the driving force behind my passion and creativity. Thank you to my grandfather, Professor Amin Mughal, for the continued heartening inspiration and encouragement.

Crossing the Raavi

Gulzar

It is a wonder that Darshan Singh did not go mad. His father died, his mother was lost somewhere in what remained of the Gurdwara, and his wife gave birth to two babies at the same time. Twins... both boys! Darshan Singh did not know if he should laugh or cry. Fate had dealt him a strange hand... taken away with one hand what she had given with the other. It was being said that freedom had come or was coming, though it was hard to tell when it would reach Lyallpur. Hindus and Sikhs were surreptitiously making their way to the safety of the gurudwara. Shahni had been moaning in pain for the last few days and nights. Those were the last days of her pregnancy and it would be her first labour.

Every day, Darshan Singh would bring a new story about the riots. Every day, his father would comfort him. 'Nothing will happen, son; nothing at all. Has any Hindu or Sikh home been attacked so far?'

'But the gurudwara was attacked, Bhapa-ji. It has been set on fire twice.'

'And yet you want to go and assemble there?'

Darshan Singh fell silent. But all around him, people were leaving their homes and gathering in the gurdwara.

'It is comforting to be in one place, Bhapa-ji. There is not a single Hindu or Sikh left in our alley. We are the only ones here.'

One night, ten or fifteen days ago, the sound of Bhapa-ji falling down in the courtyard rang out; everyone woke up. Cries of 'Jo Bole So Nihaal' could be heard in the distance, coming from the gurudwara. Bhapa-ji had, in fact, heard the shouts and woken up, and gone up to the terrace. On his way down, he had slipped on the stairs and the axe lying in the courtyard had smashed his head.

Somehow or the other, Bhapa-ji's last rites were performed; whatever little they possessed was stuffed in a pillowcase and the three of them had made their way to seek refuge in the gurudwara. There was no dearth of frightened souls inside the gurudwara. No wonder he felt buoyed with courage. Darshan Singh would say, 'after all, we are not alone; if nothing else, we are close to Waheguru.'

Groups of young volunteers would work all day long. People had collected flour, pulses and ghee from their homes. All day and all night, the community kitchen churned out meals. But how long could the provisions last…the question haunted every heart. They were hopeful the government would send some help.

'But which government?', someone would ask. 'The English have left.'

'Pakistan has been created but there is no Pakistani government in place yet.'

'I have heard that the military is all around; they are taking caravans of sharanarthis till the border under their care.'

'Sharanarthis? Who are they?' Darshan's wife asked. 'Refugees.'

'We have never heard these words before.'

'A group comprising two or three families, who could no longer bear the burden of anxiety, decided to set off.'

'We are leaving. We have heard that there are trains leaving from the railway station. How long can we sit around waiting here?'

'After all, brother, one has to find the courage. Waheguru will not carry us on His shoulders.'

Another quoted from the Granth Sahib to bolster his argument, 'Nanak Naam is the ship; he who boards the ship will sail across.'

No sooner had some people left than a bubble of emptiness would form in their absence. But as soon as a fresh set of people came with news from the world outside, the bubble would burst.

'Do you know...a huge camp has been set up at the railway station!'

'People are dying of hunger and eating stale food. Diseases are spreading.'

'Five days ago, a train had passed by this way. There wasn't space to keep a seed of sesame; people were packed even on the roof.'

The next morning was Sankrant. Verses from the Granth Sahib were being recited day and night. Shahni gave birth to her twins at a very auspicious moment. Of the two, one baby was extremely weak; it had little chance of survival, but Shahni kept it alive through the sheer force of her umbilical cord.

That very night someone said, 'A special train has come to get the refugees; let us go.'

A large mass of people set out from the gurudwara. It included Darshan Singh and Shahni too who, though extremely weak, was willing to leave for the sake of her sons. The mother refused to budge.

'I will come, son; I will come with the next lot. You leave with my daughter-in-law and my grandsons.'

Darshan Singh tried to dissuade her but the Granthi intervened. The volunteers in the gurudwara too tried to bolster his courage.

'Leave now, sardar-ji. One by one, we shall all go across the border. We will bring your mother with us.'

And so Darshan Singh set out. He put his two babies in a basket as though he were a street hawker who had set out with his family atop his head.

The train was at the railway station but there was no space inside it. People seemed to grow like grass on its roof.

People saw the weak and sickly mother and her newly born babies, pulled her onto the roof, and made some space for her.

After about ten hours, there was a small rumble in the train. The evening was red, as though bloodied, its face livid and ablaze.

Shahni's breasts were sucked dry. She would lift one baby away, then put the other to suckle. The bundle of two infants, wrapped in rags, looked like something that had been picked up from a garbage heap.

After some time, as the train slowly pushed its way into the night, Darshan Singh noticed that while one baby moved its arms and legs and even let out an occasional cry, the other was absolutely still. He thrust his hand inside the bundle and found it was stone cold.

When Darshan Singh burst into tears, the people sitting around him understood. They tried to take the baby away from Shahni but she seemed to have turned to stone too. She sat there with the basket clasped to her chest.

'No, one doesn't take milk without his brother.'

Despite everyone's efforts, Shahni refused to let go of the basket.

The train stopped ten times and moved ten times. People made conjectures in the dark.

'I am sure we have just crossed Khairabad.'

'Surely this is Gujranwala.'

'Just an hour more … as soon as we reach Lahore, it is as good as reaching Hindustan.'

And in their fervour, they began to raise slogans.

'Har Har Mahadev!'

'Jo Bole So Nihaal!'

A wave seemed to ripple through the crowd as the train climbed a bridge.

'It is the Raavi.'

'It is the Raavi! That means we have reached Lahore!'

In that clamour of noises, someone whispered something in Darshan Singh's ear.

'Sardar-ji, throw your baby here; it will find its mukti in the Raavi. What good will it do taking it across the border?'

Softly, Darshan Singh nudged the basket away from his wife. And, in one swift move, plucked the bundle out and flung it into the Raavi with a loud cry of 'Waheguru.'

The faint cry of a baby was heard in the darkness. Terrified, Darshan Singh turned to look at Shahni. The dead baby was clinging to Shahni's breast. A bubble of noise erupted all around him …

'Wagah! Wagah!'

'Hindustaan Zindabaad!'

Translated from the Urdu by Rakhshanda Jalil

Gulzar is a celebrated Indian poet, lyricist, author, screenwriter, and film director known for his works in Hindi cinema. Many collections of poems, short stories and scripts have flowed from his pen. His creative repertoire also includes plays, ballets, music albums, serials as well as books for children. His works have been translated into many languages and received national and international acclaim.

Lala Jaswant's Haveli

Mirza Hamid Baig

As the Samjhauta Express entered the Lahore railway station after getting cleared at Wagah, rushing in amidst the throngs of hawkers and porters pushing carts loaded with packets of chironji seeds and cashews, bags of paan leaves and areca nuts, and bolts of Benares silk and embroidered cloth wound in gunny sacks, he too was among them.

He had come to see his ancestral haveli and its neighbourhood in Lahore, so that on his return to Delhi, he could tell his old and infirm 'Bapu' about whether the places he had told him about existed or had changed. Bapu had made a few small requests, which he planned to fulfil.

The red tape of clearing Wagah was too tiring and he felt no pressing hurry. He stepped off the train and stood leaning on a vaulted pillar of the sprawling iron shed at the Lahore railway station, recollecting his Bapu's instructions at length.

As the train coaches were being linked at the Delhi railway station, Bapu had pressed him to report his arrival in Pakistan at a police station before doing anything else, and then to check into a nice, clean hotel near the railway station and call home informing of his safe arrival.

Yes.

Rest a little before you go out.

Yes, Bapu.

Our ancestral house isn't far from the Lahore railway station. You won't need a tonga or taxi. You can walk to the house.

Yes.

If tongas still run, the coachman will call out for Bhati Lohari. If you feel like it, take the tonga. The Railway Road branches out from the road going towards Landa Bazar and Sarai Sultan. Islamia College and Arab Hotel are on Railway Road. The same road runs from the Barafkhana square to Gawalmandi. You should get off at Dalgaran square. The rear gate to Sarai Sultan is just over there. All the buses pass through Dalgaran square and stop at Sarai Sultan. From there, they go on towards the railway station, Naulakkha, and the Do Moriya bridge.

Yes, Bapu.

Don't go towards Pathi Ground. You can go there later, if you like, but only after you have seen our house. Gujjars and cowherds live in that area. My best friend, Bala, used to live there too. Just ask at the Dalgaran square for Lala Jaswant's house. It's very close.

You should meet whoever lives there now. Do not greet them with pranam or namaste, say salam instead. Tell them that you are Lala Jaswant's grandson. If they invite you in, you should certainly stay a while and not feel shy. And then, if they allow you, have a look at the inner courtyard. In those days, there used to be a heavy wooden bed under the overhang of the veranda by the courtyard. You know, when I was small, I used to go to the school in the Ramgali area. I used to crouch on the same bedstead to do my homework on a slate. There was a well inside the courtyard, right under the common boundary wall with the neighbours. We used to throw in a pot tied with a rope to the pulley wheel from our side of the boundary, and they did the same from theirs. I used to compete against Chandu and the others to pull out the water-filled pot first. There is no need to go upstairs to the terrace. You should certainly take a look at it from downstairs in the courtyard. If the pigeons are there on the terrace, you will be able to see them. In those days, I kept shirazis, laqas and lotans as pets. Bala and Chandu kept pigeons too, copying me, and so even the neighbours' terraces could be full of pigeons. If there are any pigeons at the top of our house, just remember to ask them by the way what they give them as feed. Note down whatever they say. Don't forget it.

Yes, alright.

The house must have been allotted to a well-brought-up person. Perhaps they will invite you to stay with them, but, son, don't inconvenience them. You can stay at the hotel. Do you have money? Here, take some more.

Bapu, I have money. Please don't worry about it.

You don't have to skimp. You take it easy. Keep your passport inside your undershirt, carefully.

Yes, Bapu.

From the haveli, you should visit Rishi Bhawan too. It's right there. Let me know how well the Rishi Bhawan is looked after when you return.

Very well.

As the train engine whistled, the porters began to move faster and the noise of their loaded carts became louder.

Bapu could not speak loudly anymore but despite the great din, his voice could be clearly heard.

Son, as you leave the haveli for Gawalmandi, stop in front of the school in Ramgali, even if you just pass it from the outside. Yes, and you must take in the Arab Hotel. Many great writers and poets have frequented it. Be solemn and respectful, son.

Yes, Bapu.

At that moment, Bapu was walking along the slowly creeping train while there was clamour all around.

When you venture from the Barafkhana square towards Gawalmandi, as the crow flies, you will find a big local bookshop. If you have unspent money on the way back, pick up any old novel from there. My father was something of an atheist. You see, our neighbour Bala, and others, used to send for books from him and they used to read all kinds of books. The novels used to have many kinds of interesting titles. Just get me one of them. I have given you some of the titles to note.

Yes, Bapu. I have written everything down. Don't worry.

And, if possible, visit the Regal cinema in Cold Street. I watched Saigal and Jamuna in Devdas at the the Regal. And then there is Charing Cross on Cold Street. The zoo is on one side, the Viceroy's office on the other. Queen Victoria's huge brass statue stands at the crossroads there. The Queen will be sitting facing the Viceroy's office. I often used to walk that way during summer afternoons and rest at her feet. And I used to fall asleep there . . . and my folks . . . Bapu was repeating things which he had already heard since childhood.

. . . And, also, son . . .

But by then he was out of breath, and trying to run along the moving train, he fell behind. Craning his head, he stood out, crouching on the platform and wheezing. In the background, others who had come to say their goodbyes to passengers were waving.

Then the train gathered speed, and everything fell behind.

'Attention, please. Awam Express from Karachi . . .'

He picked up his leather bag and suitcase and made for the outside.

The loudspeaker was announcing the delay in arrival of a train from Karachi to Lahore. Before he exited the station, he showed the receipt from the visa office and found out where to report his arrival from India to Pakistan.

It was still quite bright outside and it was important to take care of this matter before sunset.

Before reaching Wagah, he had converted currency worth five hundred rupees at Atari, which was enough for his immediate expenses. He lost no time in hailing an autorickshaw and set out for the reporting centre.

When he entered the S.S.P. office, at the district court, he felt somewhat anxious as well as a little tired.

His papers were completely in order. The passport was in place. The visa was the correct one. And yet there was an inexplicable worry, as if the sky above had ceased to exist. Although he put his luggage down next to the huge desk in front of the reporting officer, taking a seat on an empty chair, he sat there like a convict.

The reporting officer glanced at him with disinterest as he continued to speak on the phone. He put the phone down, got up from the chair, and spoke coldly:

'Yes, sir. What is it?'

'I've just arrived in Lahore from Delhi.'

'OK. Show me your papers.'

The reporting officer replied and moved away. The door shut itself behind him. Now, he sat alone in the room and each moment passed with difficulty in that solitude. When the door opened after a while, the reporting officer quickly disposed of the matter.

'On your return, you must report here again. Until then all your papers shall remain with us.'

'Of course, sir. I was very worried. You're very kind. Namaskar.'

By the time he returned to the precincts of the railway station, the evening had darkened. There were hotels of different sizes, with their neon signs blinking, opposite the railway station.

He got off the autorickshaw to choose a hotel and began walking on the pavement next to the park. Many people were lying in the park at the time, receiving fist massages while the cars and minibuses going around the park appeared to throw circles of light in all directions.

'Sir, how far is the Dalgaran square from here?' He asked a gentleman, gripping the park's railing.

'It's not far at all, sir. That road in front of the hotels, the one which turns right, yes, take that one. It's just a few steps from there.'

'Alright.' And he walked on.

Bapu was right. Absolutely nothing had changed. Just a walk from the station and there was Dalgaran square. And Lala Jaswant's haveli, close to Rishi Bhawan. And all this was on the same road with the bookshop at its end point. Everything was within walking distance.

He changed more money from a money changer right in front of the hotel that he had chosen, and entered. At that moment, the clinking of bottles of oil held by the boy-masseurs in the park could be clearly heard.

The hotel room, on the second floor, was roomy and tidy. A foam mattress, heavy curtains on the windows, different taps for hot and cold water and a tiled bathroom. There are no such hotels in the area around the Jama mosque in Delhi. Perhaps only in Connaught Place. These were his thoughts as he ate dinner after having a bath.

Because of the bright lights outside and inside in the hotel lobby, he was under the impression that it was still early, but he realized it was ten at night when he glanced at his wristwatch.

It was quite late. Bapu goes to bed early, at nine. With a half-hour time difference, it would be ten-thirty in India. Realizing he hadn't called home to inform them of his safe arrival, he hurried outside. When the operator at the public phone booth gave him the line after dialling the number, Bapu was still awake.

Hello . . . hello, Bapu? Yes, I reached alright. You're still up. . . Yes, I'm fine, really. . . You were wheezing on the platform. . . how are you feeling? Yes, I went and reported my arrival. . . You were right, everything is just as it was. . . Yes, it is walking distance from the hotel. . . talk to Mother . . . Yes, I remember the road goes straight from Dalgaran square, Taj Company, Islamiya College, Arab Hotel and then the Barafkhana square and just before Gawalmandi, there is Hakim Mirza Amritsari's dispensary. . . Yes, I will remember that. . . The publishing house Dar-ul-ishaat . . . Yes, Bapu . . . I have it written down . . . I will go out in the morning . . . Yes, I will go to the haveli first thing. Don't worry. It's been a long call . . . Everything is as it was, Bapu . . . Yes, Bapu.

He put the receiver down. He had run up a huge bill.

Well, that was no problem. Bapu's worries were allayed, he thought, as he approached the hotel from the public phone booth.

When he reached the room, he locked the door and walked to the window that opened on to the railway station.

It was about eleven. The traffic on the street below had thinned and circles of light still lit up the park, but now only intermittently.

Suddenly, his gaze froze on an illuminated mountain standing in the middle of the park.

What was that?

It was a mountain lit up in the middle of the park, beside which stood a huge missile with its head pointed towards the sky.

None of this was visible in the light of day. Perhaps there were too many distractions during the day for one's eye to fall on them.

But was this mountain even there during the day? He was in a dilemma.

The mountain and the missile in the park were lit by searchlights from all four corners. And in the dim light, those who were getting fist-massages lying on bedspreads now lay unconscious and unmoving, like sacks under the lee of the mountain. The clinking of bottles of oil held by the boy-masseurs could no longer be heard.

What was this sudden manifestation? He felt disoriented.

He moved away from the window. He put off the lights and lay down on the bed.

Bapu had told him not to walk towards Pathi Ground, but he had let Dalgaran square go unvisited and so he walked towards it. School was out at the Ramgali school and all the children were playing football in the Pathi Ground. Bala! Chandu! Their mothers were calling out to them at the top of their voices to come in for lunch but the children, bathed in sweat, said that they did not want to and to let them play. Meanwhile, the buses leaving for Sarai Sultan passed one after another blowing their horns.

He awoke in the morning when the day was already bright.

After breakfast, he spoke with the hotel manager in the lobby, who informed him that the Chaghi mountain, which had changed colour during the first atomic experiment by Pakistan, was recreated in the park in front of the railway station.

Oh, he exclaimed with a deep breath.

The hotel manager gave him the names of all the famous sights in Lahore on a piece of paper. Bhati gate, Minar-e-Pakistan, the royal fort, Badshahi mosque, and several other names.

When he reached his room upstairs from the lobby to change his clothes, he began thinking that the haveli was nearby, at just a walking distance. It could be visited anytime. Let me hire an autorickshaw and visit some of these famous sights.

Also, it had become late morning. It was late March and the weather was hot. He set out in a hired auto-rickshaw.

The area around Bhati gate resembled the Jama mosque and Old Delhi. By the time he reached Minar-e-Pakistan on foot, the sun was directly overhead.

He strolled from Ranjit Singh's memorial and visited the royal fort and sat down in the Hazari garden in front of the Badshahi mosque.

Walking from the Bhati gate up to the Minar-e-Pakistan, having already visited the royal fort, he felt a little tired.

On his way back in an autorickshaw he gave up the idea of visiting Anarkali Bazar and the Punjab University. But he did feel like going to the museum.

'Brother, take me to the museum.'

As he entered the museum, he could make out Queen Victoria's huge brass statue placed inside the museum. Had Bapu visited the museum in his childhood or was this some other statue? He felt some confusion. It was a long time ago. It was quite possible that Bapu had forgotten and given him the wrong location, he thought.

'Sir, where is the Viceroy's office?' He asked a museum employee who stood nearby.

'Viceroy's office? I don't know the office you are asking about.'

I must be mistaken. I should've gone to Cold Street via Charing Cross first, he thought with regret.

No matter. I'll go straight to Charing Cross on Cold Street.

He stopped an autorickshaw outside the museum.

'Sir, I want to go to Cold Street. Take me to Charing Cross.'

'Sir? I don't know where Cold Street is. I can take you to Charing Cross. You can enquire about Cold Street there.'

'Let us go.'

It was still bright, as if a flood of light had submerged both sides of the road. When they reached Charing Cross, there was no sign of a Cold Street or the Viceroy's office. He enquired from some people in the street at Charing Cross. Anybody he asked called that road bathed in the flood of light the 'avenue of the Great Leader' or Mall Road. There was no sign of the Viceroy's office anywhere.

The zoo's existence was proven but on one side of Charing Cross was the WAPDA House's high-rise building, and on the other side the Punjab Assembly Hall. While there was a park in a triangular enclosure at Charing Cross, Queen Victoria's statue was missing and, in its place, lay a giant replica of a bookrest hewn from marble with a Quran on it, also made of marble.

He retreated from there.

He was perplexed now—if this was Charing Cross, where could Cold Street, which was flanked by dense trees on both sides be, and what became of the Viceroy's office?

Had Bapu gotten confused?

Today was not the day to call Bapu, he decided.

The disappearing of Cold Street, Queen Victoria's statue and the Viceroy's office from Charing Cross were bound to shock him.

I'll phone him tomorrow. I'll come up with some excuse. I will tell him the phone line wouldn't connect. He spoke to himself and stood confounded at Charing Cross.

During dinner in the hotel lobby, he spoke to the manager from his seat.

'Brother, I wanted to go to the Viceroy's office. I tried hard to find it, but I couldn't.'

'Where did you say you wanted to go?'

'You know, the Viceroy's office on Cold Street.'

'What office did you say? Let me find it out. But this is the first time I've heard of the name.'

The manager proceeded to ask each of the waiters on duty and remained puzzled.

'It's been seven-eight years since I've worked and lived in Lahore. But I've never heard the name of this office. Don't worry. We will find it out. Anyway, did you visit the Minar-e-Pakistan and the royal fort?'

'Yes, I did. But please find out about it. I really must go there.'

'Yes. Don't worry about it.'

At night before falling asleep, he was consoled by the thought that the next day was his visit to the haveli and the news from the haveli and the neighbourhood would please Bapu.

Before going to sleep, he set an alarm on the clock so he would not sleep in late and could return from the haveli before it got too hot.

Waking up in the morning, he did not wait. He got ready in a hurry and walked straight down to the hotel lobby. He had a light breakfast and left the hotel on the path set by Bapu.

Following Bapu's instructions precisely, he picked the Railway Road that emerged from Lunda Bazar Road, but could not find a tonga going in his direction, nor any lorries coming from Sarai Saultan towards the railway station.

It's been a long while, he thought.

Nevertheless, he came to a sudden stop many times as he walked, but it was a time when people were in a hurry and the shops along the footpath were not open. There was no one around to help him. And so, he walked on.

At a crossroads he saw a throng of people eating at a roadside cart selling naan and chickpeas and he stopped there.

'Sir, is this the Dalgaran square? I am looking for it.'

On hearing this, a heavyset man spoke good-naturedly:

'You aren't looking for it. You're already safely there. Come, in the name of God, have something to eat.'

'Well, yes, thank you. I mean . . . isn't the Sarai Sultan bus depot nearby?'

'Sarai Sultan bus depot?'

Everyone there began murmuring in surprise and they looked at each other in some amazement.

'OK, at least tell me the way to Lala Jaswant's haveli.'

'Lala Jaswant's haveli?'

Everyone murmured in amazement once more.

'OK. That's fine. Rishi Bhawan must be close by.'

'Rishi Bhawan?'

Now, everyone was staring at him.

He became flustered and started walking away rapidly.

Then, until all the shops at the crossroad opened, he kept pacing left and right, discombobulated, through the marketplace. He lost all courage to ask anyone for directions again.

He had lost all hope when suddenly, his gaze fell on a high vaulted gate abutting the overhanging roof edge of a scrapyard. On the moss-infested wall around the gate was written 'Sarai Sultan,' beneath which was an illegible date.

A wave of joy arose in his body.

He rushed towards the scrapyard, as if he had got everything he had ever wanted. Through the vaulted entrance to Sarai Sultan, inside the dimly lit scrapyard, an old man with a crooked back was busy gleaning in a heap of junk.

'Old father, isn't this Sarai Sultan?'

'Yes . . . it used to be.'

The junkman with the crooked back answered, without looking at him.

'Was this the bus depot earlier?'

'Yes, it was. In the old days.'

'I am the grandson of Lala Jaswant, old father . . . I have come from Delhi.'

'What... Lala Jaswant?'

The old junkman stopped what he was doing and turned around and drew a wicker stool in front of him to sit on.

'You see, I'm Lala Jaswant's grandson. I must see the haveli. Bapu told me that it is close to Rishi Bhawan, somewhere in the square,' he said, sitting on the stool.

'Yes. Lala Jaswant's ancestral house ... but what good is the haveli to you now? The turners occupy it now. To the left of the square you will see the pennant of the Imambara. Just before it is a turner's workshop. That used to be Lala Jaswant's haveli.'

'And, Rishi Bhawan? Where is it, old father?'

'Have some tea. You've come from afar. Would you like a Coke or Fanta?'

You're very kind but I just had breakfast. I should go now. Please continue with your work. I have a long way ahead of me, to Gawalmandi ... but you didn't tell me about Rishi Bhawan.'

'Son, I already told you ... the Imambara next to your ancestral house used to be Rishi Bhawan at one time. After 1947, the department of religious properties and endowments kept it sealed for a long time... then an Imambara came up.'

On hearing this, he stood up, but his legs felt lifeless.

'Stay a while, son.'

'No, old father ... I have some errands to run ... I must go now ... Namaskar.'

'May you live long.'

The old junkman began gleaning through the scrap heap again.

After wavering, swerving and cutting his path through the traffic of heavily loaded handcarts and smoke-spurting autorickshaws, he turned left on the square and immediately saw the Imambara.

Taking centuries to cover that short distance, he stood for a long time at the main gate of the dilapidated house next to the Imambara. Inside, the turners were bent over machines which gave off sparks: iron was slicing iron.

He stood there and cast his eyes upon Rishi Bhawan.

The black pennant was fluttering above the Imambara and the old structure looked plastered over with a coat of paint.

He turned around and started walking towards Gawalmandi through Dalgaran square. There were pigeons on the highest rooftops of a dilapidated house in front of him. Perhaps among them were shirazi, laqa and lotan pigeons.

Walking ahead, he saw the main entrance to the Taj Company which sent up a wave of happiness that sank just as suddenly. He saw an auction notice on the outer wall of the imposing edifice of the Taj Company.

Ahead on the right, Islamiya College did exist, but there was not a trace of the Arab Hotel across from it. There were two-sided shops selling galvanized pipes, sanitaryware and rubber materials, but nothing else. On enquiring, he found out that the Arab Hotel had folded up many years ago. Ramgali was just there. He turned on to it.

The same old terraces of Ramgali which were so alive in Bapu's memory were close to crashing down. He noticed a school building a little ahead on Ramgali, which was now the Muslim Model School. The building looked old.

Surely, Bapu must have gone to this school along with Bala, Chandu and the others, he thought to himself.

The school gate was closed but the bustle of schoolchildren running about could be felt outside throughout the street.

The dispensary of Hakim Musa Amritsari existed further from the Barafkhana square but no bookshop was in sight nearby or far away. He found out from the shopkeepers in the area that the previous year, the building of the Dar-ul-Ishaat-e-Punjab, which had been lying unused for a long time, had been pulled down.

In place of the Dar-ul-Ishaat stood a newly constructed shopping plaza called Hamza Centre, inside which galvanized pipes, sanitaryware and rubber sheets lay in heaps. He took in the newly constructed building from a distance so that he could describe the place to Bapu.

His eyes were then drawn towards a huge advertisement on a canvas hoarding fluttering between the outer wall of Hamza Plaza and an electricity pole. Since his Urdu was elementary, he was not able to read the entire advertisement. It said:

Come, come all to Multan!

A three-day assembly dedicated to the Prophet's rite.

Sher Shah Bypass, Sahra-e-Madina, Multan.

Caravans of the sons of Islam are on the move!

He moved his tired legs and turned back towards the hotel, reminding himself that it was time to phone Bapu.

Now, the dilemma he faced was what to tell Bapu and what not to.

He entered the hotel lobby, lost in thought.

'Today you stepped out very early in the morning. What all did you see?' The manager asked him good-humouredly.

'I made a round of all the places, Manager sahib. I'm very tired. I will retire early today. Please send me my meal upstairs.'

'I hope you are feeling well?'

'Yes, I'm alright. I'm just a little tired.' He collected the key to his room and turned to go upstairs.

He spent all day inside the room and by the time he came down again, the evening had darkened.

Seeing him, the manager gestured towards him from a distance, but he did not stop in the lobby and went straight out. When the public phone booth operator handed him the phone after dialling the number in Delhi, Bapu chided him for not calling the previous day.

'...But, Bapu, I finally visited the haveli today. Bapu, everything is as it was. Nothing has changed at all. What astonished me was that all the eminent people of Dalgaran square and Ramgali have still not forgotten Grandfather. Iqbal Gujjar, whom you remember as Bala, is alive and well. He met me with great affection. He said to me, your father must be only a few months younger than me. How could he then be old and frail? Then he prayed to God for your health...The people at the haveli are well born, Bapu. They asked me to stay with them, but I insisted on staying at the hotel...Bapu, I did go inside the haveli to the inner courtyard...But there was no bedstead under the overhang of the veranda...a lot of time has passed, hasn't it? But the well in the courtyard is as it used to be, just as you remember it...it's just that they have installed a motor pump at the well. The pigeons were there on the terrace above. And, Bapu, Rishi Bhawan is a sight to behold. There are no restrictions on prayers or religious rituals at the temple. A lot of offerings are also made there...Everything is as it was, Bapu. I will describe everything to you when I return. I will visit here and will come back in two-three days... No, I will not stay long...alright, Bapu!'

The conversation was on, but he disconnected the call.

He murmured, 'one debt paid.'

He returned to the hotel and had food in the lobby, and after chatting with the manager for a while, he went up to his room.

He ruminated from afternoon to evening and kept pacing inside the room, which tired him out. As soon as he lay down in bed, he fell asleep.

He saw that it was summertime and a dry hot wind blew from all directions. Under the deep shade of a tree-lined Cold Street and lazing about in the triangular enclosure at Charing Cross, lay Bapu on his side, in the cool shade, unperturbed whether that cool shade was cast by Queen Victoria's statue or the bookrest hewn out of marble.

Translated from the Urdu by Shad Naved

Mirza Hamid Baig is a writer of more than 35 books encompassing research, criticism, short fiction and translation. He has also contributed numerous research papers to reputed national and international research journals. He was graced with the "Tamgha-e-Imtiaz" in 2010.

The Enemy

Asghar Wajahat

Aappiji kept staring at Chintu's head and face. He stood frozen, with the scissors and comb in his hand. He had put a plank of wood on the armrests of a high chair and placed Chintu on it for his haircut. He looked at Chintu's face yet again. Chintu had taken off his spectacles, because of which his round eyes looked smaller than usual.

Aappiji knew that those in the area who called him Aappiji were actually calling him Haafizji. Nobody was to be blamed if what came out of their mouths was Aappiji, whether in haste or because they could not get the pronunciation right. A man has to leave many of his impressions behind when he leaves his home and country behind. Aappiji had come to Nareshnagar from Rai Bareilly. A well-wisher had advised Aappiji that he'd earn a lot if he opened a shop in Nareshnagar. Haafizji had come with a suitcase and set up his practice under the Neem tree. If a kind soul gave him a few extra annas, he'd return home early. Soon enough, it turned into a shop. He put a board on the shop saying, 'Hind Hair Cutting Saloon.' The reason for the shop's success wasn't just Haafizji's hard work but also the money Rahmat had sent from Karachi. All this would not have been possible without Rahmat's help. And Rahmat says that nothing would have been possible without Naseer Bhai. Naseer Bhai had financed Rahmat's move to Pakistan. Time had turned Naseer Bhai into Aappiji.

Over the years, the two brothers had quarreled many a time about moving to Pakistan. The first few discussions had been civilized. They soon turned into screaming matches. Rahmat would shout, 'Do you even know what the pay for a shave is there? Ten rupees?' Naseer, that is, Aappiji, would say, 'So, would you leave your country for Pakistan?' They would soon start abusing each other. Then, they would stop talking to each other. All Rahmat could think about was Karachi. Karachi had started featuring even in his dreams. He was running around. He hung out with the boys from the neighbourhood who had been to Pakistan and claimed that everything in Pakistan was imported. Omega watches, golden tape recorders, Gilette blades, Japanese toys...and many such things. Rahmat was also thinking about these things. His madness kept increasing. One day he said that if not allowed to go to Pakistan, he would poison himself by taking dhatura. That is when Naseer Bhai admitted defeat. He told himself that there was nothing to be done if his destiny dictated that he be separated from his brother. He remembers well the long night when he had put Rahmat in the train bound for across Khokhra. He also remembers the glorious day when Aappijji had embraced Rahmat on Pakistan's soil.

He has many bittersweet memories from the last fifty years. There were times when he was scared of mentioning that he has a brother in Pakistan. Then there were times, when dressed in clothes bought from Pakistan, he fancied himself to be General Ayyub. Every vein in his body remembers House Number 107 in D block of Naajmabad of Karachi, Pakistan—Rahmat and Zulekha's house where Sabiha and Afsana had been married. It was also the house where Rahmat's handicapped son, Adnan, sat on a chair in the verandah to look at the sky. He was twenty-seven now. Adnan could neither hear nor speak. He could not move his limbs, let alone walk. After having spent a fortune on medicines, Rahmat had now left it to Allah's will. He was of the opinion that Pakistan was created by God. Adnan was also God's creation. All they could do was be patient. Not just Rahmat and Zulekha, even the two sisters loved Adnan to bits. Aappiji was neither married, nor did he have any children. He considered Rahmat's children as his own. What was astonishing is that if there was anyone in the world Adnan recognized, it was Aappiji. Recognition flashed on his face the moment he laid his eyes on Aappiji. He could not speak but his face spoke for him. Aappiji also adored him. He had prayed for his recovery at every shrine he could visit.

Chintu had unravelled Aappiji from head to toe. Chintu was Pandeyji's daughter, Sushma's son who lived in the third lane. Chintu was always in the lanes, day or night. He was in class four but talked like he was everyone's father. For some reason, while cutting his hair today, Aappiji had asked: so Chintu, what do you want to do once you grow up?

- I'll join the army.
- Ok?
- I'll become a captain.
- What will you do then?
- I'll fight my country's enemies.
- Who are the country's enemies?
- Pakistan.
- Pakistan.
- Yes, Pakistan.

A shiver had run down Aappiji's spine and he had been struggling to brace himself. He looked at Chintu from behind his foggy spectacles. His round eyes were dancing. He knew that Chintu had learnt all this from the boys in the neighbourhood. Otherwise, how can the seven-year-old Chintu even know what Pakistan is?

- How will you fight Pakistan?
- I'll drop an atom bomb there.
- Atom Bomb!
- Yes, Atom Bomb!

Aappiji started cutting his hair little by little. But he felt his insides fill up with poisonous gas. He cleaned his spectacles again but his vision remained hazy. Then, he rubbed his eyes. He couldn't see well even after his eye ducts had dried up. He wanted to tell Chintu, Adnan lived in Pakistan. He can neither eat with his own hands nor drink. He can't walk. All he can do is see, though God only knows what he looks at. His hands and legs are not in his control. He rolls off here and there and unless someone comes and straightens him, he can't do it by himself. But he is a very sweet young man. He is fair-complexioned. The veins running through his hands are blue. His hair is black and his face is longish. He is very sweet. Yes, there are times when he has seizures. He seems to suddenly become strong. He injures himself. His wounds start bleeding. When he is at peace, he looks at flying aeroplanes. His taste buds can tell the difference between delicious and bland food. He throws up bland food.

He was thinking of telling Chintu, Beta, what will you achieve by dropping an atom bomb on a disabled man? God himself has wreaked havoc on him. He felt like an atom bomb thrown over Pakistan would drop only on Adnan. Adnan lived in God's created land and his body bore self-inflicted wounds. He made new ones even before the old ones could get the chance to heal. Meaning, he has been fighting with himself since his birth. He is a handicapped man cutting up parts of his own body, a stupid boy. He pulls his own hair with such strength that even the roots come out. He has no semblance of intelligence or wisdom. But there are times when he gets so maddened by anger that it seems like he'd butcher himself.

Chintu's hair had been cut. He took Chintu down from the chair. Sushma came. She examined Chintu's hair carefully and handed Aappiji two and a half rupees.

- Sushma! Look, your son wants to drop an atom bomb on Pakistan.
- Why! What is this nonsense you have been spewing… who taught you all this?

Sushma took Chintu's arm and pulled him outside. Still clutching the money, Aappiji sat down on the moda. The calendar with the picture of Mecca and Medina hanging on the opposite wall was swaying under the fan.

He looked at the fading picture of Rahmat on the wall. He said 'Ya Allah' to himself and started looking at the lane with haunted eyes. Before he could think of anything, Rajveer came by and said, 'What happened Aappiji, why are you looking so forlorn?'

- No, nothing, just tired.
- Tired in the morning?
- What can one say about tiredness? It can come without warning.

Saying this, he started cutting hair. But try as hard as he could, he could not think of anything but Pakistan, meaning Adnan.

He was so distracted that he cut a small pimple on Rajveer's cheek with his ustra.

- What are you doing, Aappiji? Rajveer said.
- Forgive me, Beta. I'll get an antiseptic.

Aappiji started putting some Alum on the cut but his mind was still where it had been.

Translated from the Hindi by Priyanka Sarkar

Asghar Wajahat, a retired Professor of Hindi from JMI, New Delhi is a Hindi fiction writer, novelist, playwright, film script writer. He is mostly known for his novel, *Saat Aasmaan* and his acclaimed play, *Jis Lahore Nai Dekhya, O Jamyai Nai*. He has thirty books of fiction to his credit.

Boundary Line

Naeem Baig

Spring was fading after spreading love far and wide in the air. Sabir Ali took off the binoculars from his eyes. He rubbed his bare eyes to look into the distance but the scorching sunlight blocked his vision. He raised the binoculars up to his eyes again and peeped through the lens, adjusting his gun to an upright position. The gold-tinged crops extended as far as his eyes could see. Spikes of wheat swayed in the gentle breeze, parted by a narrow trail converging into the skies along the gently flowing, murky waters of the Rohi.

He took a deep breath and looked straight ahead of him. Some fifteen feet above the ground, the tri-coloured Indian flag was fluttering in the air on a check post. Just underneath the flag, a soldier was positioned in a concrete canopy, looking through his binoculars at the green Pakistani flag fluttering over the Pakistani check post where Sabir was standing, about two hundred metres away. The other soldier on duty with him was yawning in the broad daylight.

Sabir flashed a smile at the Indian soldier, whose face reflected a strange sense of distress, perhaps because Sabir was new to him. It was Sabir's first day at this check post, though guard duty was nothing new to him. He had been accustomed to such duties. This was his first experience at the Indo-Pak border and apparently, he was relishing every moment of it. The beautiful fields were mingling with the green horizon and birds were seen flying on the east side. Large fields on the west encircled a few dwelling houses and incessant sounds of the stone-mill grinders were echoing in the air. These familiar landscapes on both sides were enough to please Sabir's heart. He randomly started humming.

The times were peaceful but the border affairs, as usual, were tense. It was a relatively calm day on both sides of the border. The weather was clear after many days of cloud cover and the visibility was unlimited. Sabir's companion was off duty for a few hours. He had taken sole charge of the check post and was absorbed in his moments of solitude.

He put aside the binoculars after keenly eyeing the surroundings and sat down on a chair placed by the four-feet high wall of the post. He turned the face of the machine-gun towards the border, and placed the gun hung on his shoulder against the wall. He opened his chest box, untied a small bag, filled the pocket of his khakis with a fist full of raisins and roasted black chickpeas, and started feasting on them. There was still an hour left before the daytime langar would be served and he was already feeling hungry.

Gorging on the chickpeas, he recalled his mother handing him over dried pudding made of granulated wheat and a mixture of raisins and roasted chickpeas before he had left his home.

'Sabir, I used to give this pudding and mixture to your father too and he would always give it to his friends. You do that too… this is for you and your friends,' his mother's voice echoed in his ears.

'Mother, if you love me so much, why did you let me join the army?' Sabir asked, patting his mother's feet.

'I've already lost your father in a war. I dread wars, my son, and I want to see peace in the world. That's the reason I am enduring distance from you,' she had talked her heart out.

'I'll do as you wish, mother,' Sabir had responded obediently.

Strange rustling sounds from the nearby bushes disrupted his train of thought. He noticed some quivering in the bushes. He raised his gun and looked a few metres away, towards the no man's land. The bushes were briskly moving, which alerted him at once. He picked up his binoculars and tried to peek into the quivering bushes. Along the markers on the boundary line, the rustling in the dry bushes grew louder, as if someone was trying to crawl on his elbows.

'Halt!' Sabir called out.

But his warning wasn't heeded. The crawling continued. After waiting for a few seconds, Sabir shouted again.

'Halt... freeze right there, or I'll shoot you.'

Sabir aimed the gun towards the bushes and removed the lock clip.

He instantly became more cautious. He lifted the binoculars up to his eyes and took a closer look at the bushes. It seemed as if more than one person was crawling in there. Bound by the rules, Sabir now had no other choice.

He shouted one last warning to halt before finally opening fire.

The thunder of the fire caused a sudden panic on the Indian side. They immediately resorted to aerial firing away from the Pakistani post.

Hearing the fierce firing from the other side, Sabir assumed that the Indian soldier must have opened the fire aimlessly in response to his fire.

Sabir raised his binoculars again and caught a glimpse of the Indian guard staring back at him through his binocular lens. Sabir indicated to the Indian soldier through a hand signal that he had opened fire at someone moving in the bushes. The Indian guard apparently understood his signal, stopped the fire and waved at Sabir to carefully look into the bushes.

Sabir had already halted the fire after the first burst. Holding his gun, he stepped down from the post. Striding closer to the bushes, he was startled to find a wounded mother dog panting in pain. Sabir's bullets had probably hit her in the abdomen. He saw two little brown puppies snuggling up to their mother, as if trying to converse with her in faint whimpers.

Sabir slung the automatic gun over his shoulder and peeked at the Indian guard through his binoculars. The Indian guard was standing on the check post, waving at him. Sabir waved back and signalled him to come down. The Indian guard was initially hesitant but gave in to Sabir's insistence. He signalled affirmation, stepped down from his post, and aiming his gun at Sabir, stopped at the Indian side of the no man's land.

Sabir was standing on his side of the no man's land. And just a few steps behind him, the dying mother dog was breathing her last. Both the little puppies looked woefully at their dying mother and at both the soldiers, whimpering through their tiny snouts. Sabir's heart welled up on watching the little puppies in such agony.

The Indian soldier pulled out a white handkerchief from his pocket and waved at Sabir as he started moving towards him. Sabir also started walking towards the Indian guard. Both the soldiers were facing each other across the barbed wire.

Both of them slung their guns over their shoulders and bent down to closely look at the puppies. Sabir bent down a bit further and picked up both the puppies in his hands. He made an eye gesture to ask the Indian soldier if he wanted to adopt one, to which he warmly nodded his head.

Sabir handed over one puppy to his Indian counterpart and held the other against his chest affectionately. He offered the puppy a handful of raisins and chickpeas from his pocket. It started sniffing Sabir's palm and chewed on the raisins. He also offered his hand to the other puppy clinging on to the Indian soldier's chest and it too started munching the raisins. Both the puppies stopped whimpering as they nibbled on the raisins.

Sabir tossed the remaining chickpeas in the air and rubbed his hands against the side of his khakis. He then drew another fist full of the raisins and chickpeas from his pocket and offered it to the Indian soldier, who accepted and gulped them down in one go.

Sabir extended his hand for a handshake and yelled out loud in a military style:

'Sabir Ali... 205 Infantry Battalion'

'Nirmal Singh... 93 Gurkha Rifles'

Both took a step back, saluted each other, and simultaneously walked back to their respective check posts.

Positioned back at his check post, Sabir caught a glimpse of the puppy tenderly moaning like a baby while looking towards him.

He lifted the puppy high over his head and called out to Nirmal. Nirmal was touched by the warmth in Sabir's voice and also raised his puppy high in the air for Sabir to see.

Clutching the puppy once again in a loving embrace reminded Sabir of his mother.

Translated from the Urdu by Dr Bina Biswas

Naeem Baig is a fiction writer best known for his hugely influential writings and essays both in Urdu and English. He has to his credit two Urdu short stories, an Urdu Novel *Deus Ali aur Diya* and two English novels titled *Tripping Soul* and *Kogon Plan.*

Paper Boats

Mohammad Atif Aleem

The eighth sun of their voyage was descending slowly into the fathomless abyss, setting the sea ablaze.

Keeping a watchful eye on each other, the fishermen's numerous boats were afloat in the landscape against the blood-red hues of the dusk. Several uninvited seagulls hovered over their heads, hoping to get their share from the fishing boats. The gradual rise of the dark was about to end another day of the voyage.

Mirani blew the last puff of smoke, dropped the still-burning butt of the cigarette into the sea and signalled to his team in the front rows of the boat to pull out the net. The fishermen secured their feet against the hull of the boat and started pulling out the net. There were a few violently wriggling fish, snakes, and shrimps in it. The observing crew threw the snakes back into the water and the fish and the shrimps onto the slippery deck. Others removed the catch from the net and stored it under the deck.

By dusk, the net was fully pulled out of the water. Mirani looked dispiritedly at the catch. The fish were much less than he had hoped for. And even in that dismal catch, there were many juvenile fish which were to grow up playing with the waves. Their lives were cut short by the harried fishermen.

Mirani looked at his comrades and decided to venture out further into the deep waters, as far as their launch could take them. But drifting into the Indian waters was a major risk. The catch was getting thinner day by day along the coastline, however, and he was ready to take that risk to fill the storage box of his boat, come what may.

The fishermen of the shanty-town of Ibrahim Haidri near Karachi all knew well that the sea was angry with them and wouldn't let them catch plenty of fish, which were their lifeline, anymore. They were also aware of the reason behind this angst—the increasing number of fishing boats with bigger and sturdier nets. Had it been only for the local fishermen, they could still get their bread and butter from the sea. The gigantic foreign trawlers that could venture deep into the high seas caused more trouble for the local fishermen by depleting the fish stocks of the sea fast. The toxic waste mercilessly dumped from the shores into the seas of India and Pakistan had further diminished the population of marine life.

As the darkness descended, Mirani, along with the captain and the crew, assembled in a circle on the wooden deck of the boat, untying their girdles. It was time to feast upon the fish-biryani and relax in the cool breeze. When the biryani was served in the aluminium pots, they forgot their miseries momentarily. The world didn't seem that bad a place to live.

Every night after dinner, using the same aluminium trays as drums, they'd hum bizarre tunes in a chorus and fall asleep on the deck, dead tired.

Mirani had slept well during the day, so he went to the stern of the boat and lit his last cigarette, looking thoughtfully at his crew members lying here and there on the deck like dead logs. As he puffed, his eyes remained fixed at the indistinct creatures shining brightly in the water. It was a dark night. The full moon was still a few days away. Stars were shining in the dark sky and appeared so near, as if they could be grabbed in the fist.

An ageing Mirani recalled his heyday, when the sea used to be full of fish and they didn't need to venture out into the deep waters to catch the fish. They would usually get back in eight to ten days with the womb of their boat full of big catch. Now, they were unable to catch any reasonable stock in a month or even more, braving the high tides. Getting back, they were hardly able to purchase even the ration and basic necessities for their families after paying off the operational expenses and half of the income to the boat owners. A few days of rest would be followed by another voyage.

Mirani was the head of a twenty-five-member crew. Of them, three were his brothers and three his sons. His fourth son, eight-year-old Shani, had insisted on coming with them to see the high seas for the first time. His nephews were also among the crew. They were all fishermen by birth. One of the nephews was hardly ten when he ventured out to the sea with his father. Many horrible memories were permanently perched in his mind, which would often haunt him as nightmares. He had seen the same tranquil sea turning violent and devouring his father in front of his eyes. Had luck not been on his side that fateful day, and a rescue vessel not picked up the remaining survivors, the savage tides would have devoured him too.

The incident left a terrifying impact on him. He never wanted to return to the sea, but as a fisherman, did he have a choice? He counselled himself to be brave and offered a hand of friendship to the sea. The sea accepted him back in its fold, like a forgiving elder and they became friends with each other again. In a few years, he had mastered the art of reading the waves, which was a must for a fisherman to venture out into the sea.

That night, precisely when Mirani was listening to the melodious voice of Lata Mangeshkar on his pocket-sized transistor, there was another boat swaying on the waves, not very far, in which Mukesh Kumar, the dweller of the fishermen's village of

Dwarka, was searching the sea for bread and butter along with his brothers, sons and other young men of his tribe.

The people on both boats shared a historical affinity and were raised by the same sea. They bore the same sparkle in their eyes as well as similar wounds in their hearts. It was hard to differentiate between them if the national flags fluttering on their respective boats were removed.

Mirani and Mukesh Kumar reached the same decision in utter desperation—to venture out further into the deep seas, come what may. So, Mirani's boat Al-Haidri turned towards the East and Dwarka Rani, the boat of Mukesh Kumar, turned to the West towards Kutch. Swaying on the waves, both the boats were getting closer to each other with every passing moment. There were several other boats, and all the fishermen were carrying the same hopes, the same despair in their hearts.

It was the twelfth day of their journey when they came across each other just before sunset. Getting this close to each other in the high seas was a routine matter for the fishermen from both countries. On the land, generations of suppression and hunger were their fate, but, in these high seas, they were the masters and the rulers. This sea was their India and their Pakistan.

All the fishermen stood up and waved at each other as they sighted the approaching boats from the other side. They feasted on the shrimp-soup and fish-biryani together, forgetting all the animosity between the two countries. This centuries-old friendship was above politics or any other barriers. The tradition of these brief encounters continued across the unseen borders in the waters—where they'd often indulge in festivities and then carry on with their nets and fishing business.

On the thirteenth day of the fruitless voyage, the crew of Al-Haidri, carrying the Pakistani flag, spotted flocks of clouds on the horizon. The harsh winds were enough to estimate that it was going to be a rough day ahead. By the afternoon, thick clouds, gathered by the winds, completely covered the sky. The waves also began to rise as the clouds obstructed the sun. The boats were fiercely swaying up and down. The omnipresent flocks of seagulls had also retreated to the safety of the shores. The boat-captain knew it would now be dangerous to stay on the sea. The gadgets they carried also assured hazard. This commotion could possibly be a matter of a temporary scare that might be over soon. They had also not received any tropical depression or cyclone warning from the shore. But the summer days on the high seas were utterly unpredictable, capable of instantly turning a smooth sailing into a horrible nightmare.

Al-Haidri's captain gazed at the waves for a while with his hands on his waist and confirmed that the western waters seemed to be in high tide, but that was not a matter of concern, at least for tonight.

Mirani saw some far-sighted captains returning while others didn't pay any heed to the early warning signals. Though the crew was not content with whatever they had caught, they suggested returning immediately. They had about two tonnes of fish stacked in their boat. It was hardly enough to make ends meet for a month. Hence, they decided to return to the shore after pulling out a few more nets till the morning.

When the night got darker, they realized their mistake of overlooking the signs. By the time they finished their supper, the ferocity of the sea could not only be seen but heard too. Furious winds were raising the waves higher and higher. And then out of nowhere, a rogue wave emerged from the north and almost turned their vessel upside down, followed by more multitudes of waves which were banging their heads mercilessly against the poor Al-Haidri. Drenched to their skin, they tried to maintain their balance on the terribly jostling boat. The cyclonic winds coming from the north weren't ready to ease down at all. With all his might, the captain helplessly tried to turn the boat. The furious winds and the mad waves pushed it towards the east where the prison of Porbandar in a hostile land awaited them.

The sight of the captain losing hope gave Mirani cold spells of fear. They were already in the proximity of Sir-Creek. If the storm didn't get pacified, they would soon be in the range of the bullets of the coastal guards of India. The same situation had haunted him in the past but this time, he had a child with him.

'Pull out the net,' he shouted, and waved to the captain to turn away the boat immediately.

All the twenty-five members of his team tried to pull out the net but to no avail. It seemed as if they were being gulped down by some sea-dragon. The furious waves made it impossible to pull out the net but instead, dragged them down into the waters. In this dark stormy landscape, the net that they called their lifeline, was now after their life. They were sure to die or at least land in the Porbandar prison, if they didn't let the net go. The tremendous pressure made it hard to cut off the ropes, and neither was it possible to untie the knots.

Mirani raised his hands in the sky, seeking divine help. His eyes were shut and his lips recited prayers. He got distracted by a loud horn of a bigger vessel. Blinded by the beams of heavy flashlights, he barely saw a bigger vessel carrying the emblem of the Indian navy approaching them fast.

2

To divert the attention of the people, the media on both sides of the border was continuously flashing news about the arrest of scores of suspected terrorists by the Indian Coast Guards and the Maritime Agency of Pakistan, who were behind bars now. But they didn't deem it necessary to say how many weapons and suicide jackets were recovered from these terrorists and what was the magnitude of destruction that was averted by the arrest of these people.

Far from the media frenzy and the official complexities, in Porbandar prison of India and in the Landhi Jail of Pakistan, Mirani and Mukesh could barely remember when and why they had been put behind bars. The only thing in their mind was the humiliating way in which they, the sons of the seas, were blindfolded and handcuffed behind, as if they were the biggest threat to regional and international peace.

So many were stuffed in a small, hot and humid prison cell whose ceiling fans were removed just before they were moved in. They weren't properly fed, let alone given any other facility. This was Mukesh's first time in a prison, but Mirani had been through all that before. He was certain that they weren't the masters of the sea but merely chained slaves caught frequently by the governments on both sides just to settle their scores—later forgotten to rot in the prison cells. He knew they were here at least for four to five years, if not more, and they could even die in this very cell. He was aware of everything, except how the people they had left behind would live their lives without them.

How to live without them?

This very question was also haunting Mai Hajiani, the aged mother of Mirani and Usha Rani, the wife of Mukesh. They could not single-handedly feed their respective households. They could not earn enough to get the provisions even for two days by mending the tattered fishing nets and repairing the shanty-huts in the village.

They had no idea what happened to their loved ones out in the high seas. Had they been devoured by the savage sea, or were they still alive and rotting behind the bars in the prison of the enemy country? Nobody from any side had informed either of them about the fate of their men. A few words from a telegram would have given them hope, but that never happened.

On one end, there were the desolate shores of Ibrahim Haidri and on the other the terrifying endless expanses of the shores of Dwarka, where two shadows would stroll daily, one tapping her stick and the other barely dragging on her sick skeletal frame. Both would keep on gazing at the far horizon across the sea till the fall of the night. They were strangers to each other but mysteriously well aware of each other's presence, as the sea breeze carried their whiffs across the border. They both felt each other's presence, sitting at two different places along the same stretch of the shore.

Since Mai Hajiani behaved strangely most of the time, the people in the village ridiculed her for losing her senses ever since her sons and grandsons had disappeared. One day, she did a weird thing. She tore some pages from the notebook of her grandson, who had left school to work as a labourer, and made many paper boats out of them. On a gloomy evening, she came to the shore with those paper boats in her hands. Somehow, she knew that her other self, Usha Rani, on the shores of Dwarka, was also there with the paper boats in her hands.

When both women belonging to different parts of the world got tired of standing still and gazing far into the horizon, they left the paper boats on the waters and placed in them a small note with a message.

Many years have passed but the two paper boats are still afloat, journeying towards each other from opposite directions, braving the high tides and the ferocity of the seas.

Translated from the Urdu by Dr Bina Biswas and Abdal Ahmed Jafri

---

Atif Aleem is a fiction writer, poet, a non-fiction writer, and a translator. He has to his name two Urdu fiction novels: *Mushkpuri ki Malika* and *Gardbad* and two collection of short stories: *Shamshan Ghast* and *Shehar-e-Namatloob.*

Love During Armistice

Anirudh Kala

Prakash awoke with a start. It was neither the rain hitting the asbestos sheets the roof was made of, nor the sharp crackle of firewood, that had disturbed his sleep. It was a more definite sound, like a scrape and rustle. Jasmeet, next to him, continued to sleep undisturbed. They were in a cottage in a remote hilly area beyond Simla. Barefoot, he tiptoed over the wooden floor into the tiny sitting area, now filled with a mellow glow from the embers in the fireplace. He picked up Jasmeet's shawl that was flung onto the back of a chair and wrapped it around his shoulders. He found his slippers and, bracing himself for a chilly draft, carefully opened the door a few inches. The black gleam of his motorbike, visible by the dim light in the awning, reassured him. The two of them had driven up the hills from Chandigarh for a weekend getaway at Kufri, refusing to be browbeaten by the certain prospect of rain. The nurses' grapevine at the hospital had, of course, ratcheted up their relationship several notches. Prakash was a resident in Psychiatry and Jasmeet, a trainee psychologist there.

What startled him was the sight of a young boy in school uniform lying face down on the seat, with his head on the handlebar, hands dangling by his sides and feet in drenched canvas shoes touching the muddy ground at awkward angles. Prakash, anxious and annoyed, patted the boy hard on his back. The white shirt was sopping wet. The kid squirmed and managed to straighten himself with difficulty. He looked perplexed and then surprised to find himself where he was. He wiped dribble with the back of his arm from a youthful round face with very short crew-cut hair, a style favoured by school headmasters in the hills.

'Who are you?' Prakash asked gently, trying not to sound offended.

'Brij Bhushan, 11B', the youngster in wet clothes said mechanically, gathering his school bag from the floor, where it had left a puddle.

'I mean, what are you doing here?' Prakash said, tapping his wristwatch. It said 11.30 p.m. 'At this time? In this weather? Didn't you go home after school?'

There was no reply. Brij seemed not to have heard him. The rain was creating quite a racket now. He strapped the dripping school bag to his back and looked ready to walk back into the sheets of rain.

'Wait! Go after the rain stops. You can come in and wait.' Prakash, on an intuition, stopped himself in time from adding 'we can call your parents.'

Brij halted uncertainly at the edge of the veranda. Instinctively, Prakash stepped forward to steer him by the elbow through the door before he walked away. He gathered up the clothes strewn across a chair next to the fireplace, indicating Brij should sit there. Brij took off his wet school bag, placing it in a corner of the room on the floor. He prised open the wet knot of his school tie, pulled it open, and laid it neatly on the top of the bag. Prakash asked him to take off the mud-spattered shoes and the wet socks too. The young man sat at the edge of an easy chair, gingerly at first, then rested his head on the back of the chair and within moments, comforted by the warmth from fireplace, was fast asleep. Prakash watched over the childlike face and touched the forehead with the back of his hand. It felt hot despite being wet. He went to the bedroom and woke up Jasmeet, 'We have a young visitor, and he has fever.'

Jasmeet, always the more pragmatic one, took charge. She opened the school bag and took out a damp exercise notebook which informed them that Brij Bhushan studied at DAV School, Simla. Suppressing a yawn, she dug into the school bag again and came up with a school diary with a red plastic cover. It had his father's name, a home address in Lower Bazaar, and a phone number. She picked up the receiver of the dial-less black phone lying on the mantelpiece above the fireplace and gave the number to the receptionist, who offered to shift the boy to the main hotel building, half a kilometre away, till the family came. She also offered to see if a doctor could be found at that hour. Jasmeet looked at the calm face of the boy asleep, thought about the fever and the rain, and said that it was not necessary and, looking sideways through a gap in her long hair, added that her husband was a doctor.

Telling Prakash to add some wood to the fire, she went through the pantry door to heat milk which she had saved for the morning tea, took out two tablets of Crocin from her purse and asked Prakash to wake up the kid. Brij got up, again looking confused about his surroundings, but dutifully took the medicine. His clothes had started to dry already. Prakash rinsed the glass in the pantry and came back to take the third chair.

Jasmeet asked him, 'How did you reach here from Simla?' Having travelled on the same route a few hours earlier, she knew that it was twenty-five kilometres on a high mountainous road, with deep ravines on one side.

'I walked. I do it often.' Brij said airily, as if that part was the least important. Anticipating the question about weather, he said, 'I stopped on the way when the rain was heavy. I had left early.'

'After school?' Jasmeet enquired.

The boy nodded. 'My father beats me. He would have beaten me today also.'

'Why?' Jasmeet asked, trying to put on a brisk, professional tone.

'Because I write letters. I wrote one today too. The English teacher took it away and told my father on the phone.'

'What is wrong with writing letters? I write letters all the time. Is it a girl that you write to?' Jasmeet asked, trying to sound casual, as if she was talking about weather while pretending to be busy with the fireplace. Brij kept quiet. His hair having dried, his face was looking a bit more like a grown up's. He fidgeted under Prakash's gaze, fussing with the brass buckle of his belt, which carried what looked like a school insignia, with two stiff flags in red and blue. Prakash got up to make coffee.

Jasmeet justified to herself the protective tenderness she was feeling for the boy with the unclouded face and delicate features, by telling herself it was fine; she was not in the clinic. 'What is her name?' she asked, trying to comb her hair with her fingers.

Brij looked at her, for the first time with a trusting expression. 'Benazir,' he said simply.

Jasmeet, with the air of someone who has finally discovered the key piece in a jigsaw, took the cup of black coffee that Prakash offered her and said, 'So she is a Muslim? And that is why your father does not want you to write to her? Is she in your school?' Brij shook his head slightly and Jasmeet presumed that it was in response to her last question about whether the girl was in his school, and not the earlier ones.

The hotel and its cottages lay scattered on a hillock, a couple of hundred feet above the highway, and any vehicle which laboured up the steep road at that hour, particularly if one remembered the Indian car engines of the early seventies, was bound to be heard from far now that the rain had stopped. Brij was suddenly alert and blurted accusingly, 'You called my father!'

Prakash tried to explain, 'You are running a fever. What were we supposed to do? You should be home in bed anyway.'

Sensing a trap, his eyes now deep with suspicion, Brij darted for his schoolbag and shoes. The tie and socks slid to the floor as he rushed to open the door. He turned back and asked Jasmeet politely, without any rancour, 'Was the milk poisoned?'

Jasmeet, who had got up to plead with him not to go out, was taken aback. As she fumbled for a response, the door was flung open and a harried middle-aged man in a turtleneck sweater burst into the room and ran into Brij.

'Oh, I am so sorry,' he apologised profusely for having come in without knocking. The tired-looking visitor went back to the door to take off his wet chappals, glaring all the while at Brij, whose gaze seemed to now be riveted to a spot on the floor.

'Please sit. He had fever but he is better now,' Prakash said.

While taking the chair vacated by his son, Sunil Kant Behal explained that he owned a small cafe in Lower Bazaar and lived above it with his wife and two sons. The elder boy worked with the father. He concluded with another bout of apologies for having caused so much trouble through his good-for-nothing younger son. Prakash said reassuringly, 'Please do not apologize. There is no need.'

The embarrassed father replied, 'Of course there is. He ruined your night. You are obviously here on holiday, not to nurse truant boys who invite fever by walking for hours in the rain. It is not the first time I have had to apologize on his account. It has become a way of life for me. I am an expert at apologizing. Apologizing and collecting him from all sorts of places at odd hours is all that I have been doing these last two months,' he finished bitterly.

He looked self-consciously at the fingers of his right hand, smeared dark with grease, and explained, 'The carburettor got stuck. I forgot my handkerchief in a hurry.'

Jasmeet looked at the lines on the unshaven, hassled face and invited him to wash his hands at the washbasin in the pantry. When he returned, he looked at Brij and asked acidly, 'Shall we go home? Unless Behal Sir has some more urgent business to attend to around the hills. It is only one in the morning yet.'

Jasmeet had hesitated to intervene between father and son, but a look at the boy's stricken expression made her feel protective, 'He does not go home because you beat him up for writing letters to a girl. Apparently, she is a Muslim. You should instead sit with him and talk.'

With Brij still standing in the corner biting a nail, Sunil turned in his chair to confront Jasmeet and said, 'Did he also tell you that he has written forty letters in two months?' Then, more in pain than anger, '"Apparently Muslim girl" indeed! Is that what he told you? Do you know who the girl in question is? Benazir Bhutto, daughter of President Bhutto of Pakistan!'

For a moment, Jasmeet dismissed this as a private joke between father and son. Prakash, bringing coffee for Sunil, stumbled at the pantry door, 'Has he seen her pictures in the newspapers?' This was long before television came to Simla.

'He has seen her once. On Mall Road. It was two months back, when she was here with her father for the Simla Agreement.'

Prakash and Jasmeet had stopped at a restaurant in Simla on their way to Kufri. The walls were full of photographs and newspaper cuttings related to the recent India-Pakistan summit. There was even a photograph of the restaurant owner beaming proudly with some journalists from Pakistan who had visited his restaurant for coffee. In the wake of a fierce war which the two countries had fought six months earlier, a summit was an urgent necessity, particularly for Pakistan. It had not just lost the war, but also half the country. East Pakistan, separated from West Pakistan by two thousand kilometres of Indian landmass, had declared itself independent Bangladesh after India had forced a surrender by the Pakistani army.

Sunil, leaning forward in his chair, looked at Brij and then at Jasmeet with eyes full of hurt and asked plaintively, 'When will the Partition of the two countries leave us alone? In front of my eyes, I lost my father to it, when I was that old,' he said, nodding at Brij. 'And now my son.'

A piece of wet wood had begun smoking. Prakash added fresh wood, stoked the fire and opened the outer door just a bit. Jasmeet, trying to hold down her cough, asked 'What has Partition got to do with it? It was twenty-five years back. Aren't you stretching the point?'

Sunil said lamely, though with tears in his eyes, 'If there was no Partition, there would have been no war and no Simla Agreement.' He added bitterly, 'She came to free her prisoners and condemned my son to the life of one.' Leaning against the wall, Brij gazed expressionlessly at the wooden beam in the ceiling. Prakash, now standing with his hands on the back of Jasmeet's chair, asked Sunil, 'What exactly happened?'

'You see, when the Pakistanis were here for four days, Simla was decked up like a bride. Everybody was excited. The summit was happening just six months after we won the war. Ninety thousand Pakistani prisoners of war were still in Indian custody, telling their families across the border, day in and day out on the radio, about how they were safe and well looked after by their Indian captors,' Sunil explained, trying to rub off another stubborn grease stain he had discovered on his wrist. 'The Indian government prolonged the charade deliberately. When the Pakistanis landed here for a compromise, we could afford to be magnanimous. Combine that with the ever-gushing Punjabi sentimentality and the social graces of the Pakistanis, you had

Simla fawning over the delegation, particularly the father and the daughter, as if they were long-lost relatives. Shopkeepers called her their daughter and refused to accept money for her shopping.

'She chatted with some Indian students of her age, standing on the Mall Road in front of a cafe, to make it look impromptu, although it was of course orchestrated. The whole road was cordoned off.' Sunil looked at Brij, who was standing with his back against the wall staring vacantly at the fire. 'Our Brij here tried to pass through the cordon and got pushed around because he insisted on joining the group. As an angry commando lifted his hand to hit him, Benazir, who spotted the commotion, gestured to the soldier to let the boy go. Just then, the government minders decided that she had had enough interaction with Indian university students for the day and whisked her away.'

'But what happened during those few seconds was enough for Mr Brij Bhushan Behal of DAV School, Lakkar Bazar, Simla to conclude that Kumari Benazir Bhutto, daughter of Shri Zulfikar Ali Bhutto, President of Pakistan, was head-over-heels in love with him. He is sure she had been for a while, even before leaving for India, even when she did not know that he existed... not that she now knows that he exists.' Brij's face had become smaller with every word spat out by his father. He sat slumped on the wooden stool lying near the door, with his head resting against the wall, his hands in his lap.

Jasmeet, who had been struggling not to seem judgemental, dropped all pretence. She looked at Sunil blurting angrily, 'You do not make it easy for him, do you? I think you are half the problem!'

'What have I done?' Sunil looked hurt.

On familiar territory now, Prakash gestured at the two of them to calm down. He looked at Brij, who had appeared to be briefly interested in the proceedings when his father was being scolded.

Far away, a clock struck two. It was probably the church. Prakash and Jasmeet had stopped in the afternoon to take pictures of the quaint cemetery where hundreds of British army men lay nestled against the pine-shaded mountain slope, under crumbling gravestones behind a church. He wondered in passing why he had not heard the clock before; perhaps the wind had changed direction, or the rain had stopped? Brij continued staring into the flames as if he had not heard the question.

Sunil answered Prakash, studiously avoiding looking at Jasmeet. 'She comes into his dreams and tells him secrets which even her father does not know. For instance, what she was going to wear the next morning, when she was in Simla.'

'Didn't I know beforehand that she was going to wear the silk sari with flowers at the function?' Brij asked his father angrily, suddenly feeling a need to defend himself, now that he was being ridiculed before strangers. 'She said she had not told her father yet, and she was telling me!'

'Well, if you knew, you kept it to yourself till even I knew from the pictures in the newspapers.' Sunil reminded him.

'I scratched it on a rock at the Jakhu hill. It is still there. Go and see. She even told me about the black shirt and cream bellbottoms.' Brij's fever seemed to have gone. He was willing to argue point by point with his father, especially after noticing that the charming lady with the long hair was on his side.

'And you scratched that bit about bellbottoms too, on a rock in the hills? Who knows when? I have no problem with whatever madness it is, as long as it stays in your dreams. She is gone in any case. My problem is the police and the snooping detectives who come every time you write a letter to her. The whole of Lower Bazaar comes to know that there has been another letter. Shopkeepers taunt me by asking when they should expect to go to Pakistan with the baraat. Should they ask the tailors to start stitching new dresses…tailors take time, you see, one jeers. Another one laughs asking, "Is it true that the bride is older than the boy by two years?"'

'Brij quarrelled a lot with his classmates throughout those days,' Sunil looked at Jasmeet and continued in a gentler tone, 'because the boys were unhappy with so much affection being ladled out to people from an enemy country. Boys are like that, you know, and the war had been so recent. I say, we went overboard as hosts. The government barred the public from the Ritz theatre for three days. The Pakistani guests wanted to watch *Anarkali*, *Mughal-e-Azam*, *Chaudhvin Ka Chand* and whatnot. Mall Road was barricaded because the Pakistanis were coming to shop and sample Guruprasad's paan. The schoolboys resented this, and Brij was roughed up when he argued with them about the duties of a host. He had to be given stitches on his forehead. Another time, when he waxed eloquent about Benazir Bhutto's grace and dignity even with her country in such a humiliating position, the boys made fun of him. He came home and hit his brother over a trifle. Twice, the police brought him home because he was found loitering around the Governor's house. He told me later that "she" had called him there.'

The door blew open because of the wind and then banged itself shut. Prakash got up to bolt it. The electricity went off. Brij's face glowed in the light from the fireplace, 'Papa, what should I do? It is true. It is true!' With that, he started crying helplessly.

There was the hum of a generator starting somewhere above them on the hill, and the tube light flickered back to life. Sunil looked at his watch and got up with a start. He apologized all over again, profusely thanked them with folded hands, took Brij by the hand and carrying the school bag and tie in his other hand, went out. Prakash and Jasmeet came to the door.

The rain had stopped but it was still very windy. Sunil's Fiat refused to start. He sheepishly waved, as if requesting them to return inside. He tried a few times more and then, as if re-enacting a practised drill, Brij jumped out briskly, went to the rear, pushed the car, his head down and cheeks puffed out. When they reached a downward slope, he ran back to get in, as Sunil pulled back the handbrake. As the car glided down and the engine spluttered, Jasmeet pulled Prakash into the cottage, laughing, 'So much for our first night out together.'

They stayed in Kufri for two more days but did not come across Brij or his father again. They even went to Lower Bazaar because Jasmeet wanted to buy glass bangles, without seeing any sign of them. They did not particularly look for the café because it was getting late, and the weather was worsening.

A year passed, during which Prakash would remember the stormy night in the Simla hills and their besotted young visitor whenever he saw a news report about Zulfikar Ali Bhutto.

Prakash was the duty resident at the Post Graduate Medical Institute in Chandigarh. One night, when a student nurse dropped the case files of the day's new admissions on his table, he read the large bold letters, 'Brij Bhushan Behal.' It was him all right, with the correct father's name and the Lower Bazaar, Simla address. The meticulous history written in the outpatient form mentioned the Simla Agreement as the 'precipitating factor'.

It went on to describe at length the 'patient's preoccupation with Benazir Bhutto to the exclusion of everything else' and 'a delusional belief that she visits him in dreams and the two have long conversations… The patient firmly believes that Benazir Bhutto loves him, but because of her father being the Prime Minister of Pakistan and the two countries being bitter enemies, cannot admit it openly: hence the nocturnal visits. For some months, after the onset, the patient used to write frequent letters to her, care of Radcliffe College, Cambridge, MA, USA. The patient says that this address was given to him by her in one of the dreams. This happens to be the correct address, according to the patient's father, who thinks that he may have read it in a magazine. The letters were intercepted by the police who came to investigate each time.

'However, he stopped writing to her because now she "visits" him frequently and letters are "no longer needed". The patient is also aware that she has recently moved to Oxford University in UK. He says this too was told to him by BB, the initials by which he refers to her fondly. He says that they happen to be his initials too, and she also calls him by the same name. He admits when asked that he does not have access to her dreams. When pressed for the reason, he says that the Department of Dreams is much stricter that side, but she is trying to procure the code for him.

'Always a sober, studious student who used to get excellent grades, the patient failed his higher secondary examination and managed to just pass it the following year. Both he and his father were keen that he join college, but by then, everybody in the town knew about his "problem" and no college in Simla agreed to admit him.

'The patient was taken to a local psychiatrist who advised rest and medication. However, the father stopped the medicines, when one night, Brij was found walking on the Sanjauli highway in a groggy condition. He barely escaped being run over, according to a tea stall owner. Brij was taken to another psychiatrist who advised a different medication which worked and made the "dreams" much less, but which the patient refused to take for that very reason.

'The patient says that he and Benazir often have long political discussions which range from friendly banter to heated arguments. When asked for an example, he mentioned that she was miffed with him for insisting that Kashmir belonged to India. The patient had argued that although the majority of the population of Kashmir was Muslim, it had a Hindu king who had signed the accession treaty with India. She, according to him, angrily countered that Junagarh had a Muslim king who had signed an accession treaty with Pakistan, but the state was still forcibly occupied by India, with the argument that the majority of Junagarh's population was Hindu. The patient thinks that she has a point because you cannot look at the religion of the king in one state and the religion of the population in another state for deciding which way the state should go.

'He also laments on her behalf that the ninety thousand prisoners who India had promised to release have still not been freed a year after the Simla Agreement. The patient angrily insists that this amounts to breach of trust.'

There was more about how the patient had recently started to stay out for days, after his mother casually mentioned that she would like to get the two sons married at the same time. He would roam the hills day and night, in rain and sleet, and would come back on his own in a dishevelled condition, often sick with cough and fever. The family, according to the out-patient resident, had started to show signs of 'carer fatigue' and had stopped looking for him when he went away.

Prakash looked for the bed number on the file. It was of one of the private rooms down the corridor. Patients in the rooms slept earlier than those in the ward, so he walked quietly to see if Brij was awake. The light was switched off, but the door was open a couple of inches. In the light from the corridor, he saw Sunil and Brij in a deep sleep in the same bed, with Brij's arm thrown carelessly around his father. Prakash smiled and thought that Benazir Bhutto still had some work to do. He was wrong.

The next day, Prakash left the hospital early. He had to catch a train to Delhi for a seminar. When he returned after three days, he was told by a wide-eyed breathless student nurse that the boy from Simla who had 'delusions of erotomania' had absconded from the hospital. For three consecutive nights, he had not had his dream, and he blamed the treatment.

Another two years went by without news of Brij. Prakash remembered the young boy from the hills with his unusual malady only when coming across news about Pakistan. Then, one early winter morning, as he was coming out of Delhi airport, tired and spent after a much-delayed flight from Europe, a man in a long coat and a Kullu cap stepped forward from the row of people waiting to receive their relatives and stood in front of him, looking as surprised as Prakash himself. It was Sunil Kant Behal. He had come to receive his elder son, who was returning from Switzerland after completing a course in hotel management. Prakash pulled his trolley out of the way to talk to him. He asked him about Brij and was told that he had not been seen after the night he ran away from the hospital, two years ago.

'Do you know anything about his whereabouts?' Prakash asked.

'Someone I know saw him in Ajmer last week. Brij said he had been waiting for a special guest from Pakistan, somebody who had told him about coming to Ajmer Sharif, not through a letter or a telegram, but in a dream.' Sunil's attention was drawn by his elder son coming towards them from the airport entrance. As he waved, Prakash asked,

'Are you sure it was him? There are many people like that at dargahs. Did your friend know him?' 'No, my friend did not know him, but it was him all right. He had a tattoo on his arm which read "Brij Bhushan Bhutto."' Sunil tossed his head over his shoulder as he went forward to receive his elder son and usher him through the crowd.

Anirudh Kala lives in Ludhiana and is a psychiatrist and a writer. His interests include intergenerational effects of Partition of India.

A collection of interconnected short stories, *The Unsafe Asylum: Stories of Partition and Madness* was published by Speaking Tiger Books in 2018. A novel, *Two and a Half Rivers* about a young Dalit couple caught in the vortex of terrorism in Punjab in the nineteen eighties has been published recently by Niyogi Books.

A Snowful Desire

Saeed Ahmed

'Mother, I want to go fetch some snow from the mountains!' he would urge when I'd put him to bed.

'Yes, son, but look at the blanket of stars in the skies. We will wrap it around ourselves and fall asleep.'

I would try to draw his attention to the stars and sleep-fairies but he would insist on listening to the stories of the snow-capped mountains.

'Look there! A fairy in a gaudy attire is descending from a magical star-studded milky way, just for you.'

'Munnu, my darling, the fairy is filling up your eyes with sleep.'

But he would drowsily ask, 'When will father take me to the mountains?'

I would keep looking at him as he'd fall asleep, patting him gently and kissing his forehead and eyes. His eyelids would be tightly shut but I would still see his eyes shining through them. His eyes were the most beautiful feature on his face. I would often shudder at the thought of someone's evil eye harming him.

But then, I would laugh at my own thoughts. Every child is the most beautiful in the eyes of their mother. Lost in the maze of my thoughts, I would gradually drop off to sleep.

Waking up to the morning call to prayer, I would catch the sounds of splashing water drawn from the hand pump by Mian Ji for ablution. I would kiss my son's eyes and forehead before getting out of bed.

Two red bricks were placed, one on top of the other, against a cracked wall across the charpoy. Stepping on them, my son would fix his gaze for hours on the two snow-capped mountains gleaming at a distance in the sunlight. I would repeatedly call him for breakfast but he would not bother until he'd be dragged down from upstairs.

Looking at the snow-covered mountains from his rooftop in the scorching heat for hours had tanned his skin. But he would take no heed of our complaints. His father, Master Siddiq Ahmed, slapped him a few times and locked him up in the room. He took to his grandfather's prayer mat pleading with God to send his father away from their home. God also promptly answers the prayers of children. The next day, his father was transferred to the city from the village. He was promoted to the position of a high school teacher. Elated at the news, he immediately packed up and off he had gone. Munnu was now as free as a bird.

He would spend hours on the rooftop in the blistering sun, looking at the mesmerizing mountains. Hearing the call from the street, he would sprint down to grab and gorge on the ice lollies dipped in green and red sugary syrup. He would get even more ice from the bazaar to chew on and would drink ice-cold water. That's all he would do all day.

I could only climb up the steep staircase a few times a day to bring him down. His father was in the city. His grandfather was old. So, Munnu remained engaged in his favourite pastime of watching the mountains. I would sometimes wonder about the other kids in the neighbourhood. Why did only Munnu have such unusual fascinations?

In the morning, he would often touch his eyes with raween flowers and kiss the pomegranate flowers. The fragrance of the night-blooming jasmine would intoxicate him and I would save him from falling. Watching him, I'd often wonder why unusual things would impact him so strongly. I would often ask him but he'd not find words to express. Frown lines would appear on his forehead as he would plunge into deep thoughts but still be at a loss for words.

His father was also worried about him. He would fail to comprehend Munnu's fascination with the snow-capped mountains, for which he would tolerate the scorching heat of the sun. Covering his head with a towel soaked in ice-cold water, he would look at those mountains. His father had once mentioned his condition to a doctor friend and I got terrified when he said, 'Munnu is a hyper- sensitive child. He needs extra attention and care.'

He had been given tender affectionate care ever since he was born. Looking at him on the day of his birth, his grandfather had said, 'He's illuminated our house.' He named him Munawwar (the illuminated one) and prayed, 'May God always protect him. His luminous face has lit up our village. There is one moon in the sky but he has got two....his eyes.'

A strange sense of fear often took hold of me. Afraid of my own thoughts, I would sometimes feel like a startled fawn. I tried my best but the distressing thoughts kept returning.

One fine day when I had had enough, I went straight to the post office. Unable to contact Munnu's father after several phone calls, I telegrammed him to come home immediately.

His father was surprised to see how Munnu rushed and embraced him tightly. 'Father, I have decided. We will use the kite string to hook it up to one of the mountains and drag it down to our home. You and I, right?' he asked.

Master Siddiq felt the ground slipping under his feet when his wife told him about their son's condition. Munnu's eyes had turned so red that drops of blood could be seen tangled in them. The redness reduced when Mian Ji recited some verses and blew on his eyes. Master Siddiq brought a friend's motorbike to take him to the mountains. The motorbike rushed through the dirt tracks between the fields, leaving behind thick black spiralling smoke from its silencer. Munnu had snugly wrapped his arms around his father, sitting behind him on the bike. But his father would feel a rush of panic whenever Munnu would free his hands to clap with joy.

Munnu could see that the mountains were gleaming in the sun just in front of him. Master ji parked the motorbike. Munnu got off and sprinted towards the mountains. A thick wall of barbed wires blocked his way. 'Father… let's move ahead.' Master Ji's voice choked as he hugged Munnu tightly.

Both the father and son sat down by the barbed wire. Munnu's eyes had turned bright red from weeping endlessly. He could see sparrows, pigeons and crows flying around freely. His heart ached as he wanted to fly like those birds. He rushed once again towards the barbed wire. Master Siddiq pulled him and held him closely against his chest.

'You were born here. This is your country. I was born across that barbed wire… but that is not my country anymore.'

'You are lying, father… take me to the mountains. I will make a house out of the snow. That will be my house.' Master Siddiq was utterly despondent. 'Where, where, my son?'

When they got back, Munnu immediately headed upstairs to the rooftop. Master Ji entered the room and stood against the wall. It was a dimly lit room where two of us stood, gazing down, neither looking nor talking to each other. We were not even sure whether we were alive or dead.

Hearing a loud scream, we hastily rushed outside like people run towards the doors during an earthquake. We collided with one another and collapsed.

Mian Ji stood close to Munnu who was lying unconscious on the ground.

'He came to my room crying and said that he could not see the mountains….' said Mian Ji as his lip quivered.

In the gloomy room of the doctor's clinic in the city, Munnu curiously asked, 'Father, night has fallen, but why aren't there any stars?'

The doctor laughed and responded, 'Look here, son….' And in the blinding beam of the torch, dancing stars appeared before Munnu's eyes.

While examining Munnu, the doctor light-heartedly probed 'Master Ji, why don't you take him to the mountains?'

Stupefied, Master Ji tried to collect his words and remarked, 'Doctor saheb, those are the mountains of Jammu & Kashmir.'

'And your village is?'

'Karmo Wali, Doctor saheb, at a distance of about three kilometres from the border.'

'What's his date of birth?'

'August 1947. He's seven years and ten months old.'

The doctor called Master Ji over to the other room.

'Mother, I want the candle that the doctor is holding. I can see the stars, the mountains and the snow in its light,' Munnu requested wishfully.

'Mother, mother, why don't you speak...,' he repeated.

Munnu was fast asleep on our way back to the village from the city. I helplessly raised my hands in the air and prayed, 'O God! Why can't you just make the mountains move and come to this side of the border?'

A blood-soaked smile appeared on the grim face of Master Siddiq, that almost turned into the shape of a barbed wire. The border ripped apart the bust of the land. The sun came out and melted the snow from the mountains. And the light poured out from the eyes of the child.

Translated from the Urdu by Bina Biswas

Saeed Ahmed is a distinguished playwright, writer and journalist. He has been penning drama serials for Pakistani TV channels since 1994. His critical appreciation of films includes a book on Dilip Kumar's contribution to Indian cinema. He is also well known for his political satire, including his popular lampooning of the military dictator Zia-ul-Haq. As a script consultant, he has worked on some major South Asian projects including Nandita Das' film 'Manto'.

Mehdi Hassan in Vienna

Ashok Pande

I first saw the old gentleman at an open market in Ottakring, selling inexpensive woollen jackets of the kind made in Jalandhar and Ludhiana. For ages, people from Turkey settling in Vienna have chosen to live in Ottakring, and it has traditionally been the district for wage-earners and labour hands. Of late, many immigrants of Asian descent have also started to reside here. The market in this locality of Vienna, known to be one of the most advanced cities in the world, gives the impression of an old world, resembling pictures of Kabul or Istanbul. I had been there on business for the past three months. It was late October. Winter was in the air. The streetlights were on as early as four-thirty or five. I was scheduled to return to India next month. I wanted to invite my European friends to dinner some evening before I made the trip back home. Beautiful Cornelia, who had arrived from Romania to study music history, had wished to taste biryani, having heard a lot about the exotic dish.

I had heard about the market and the old gentleman from an acquaintance. He would put up shop every week in the open market. Nobody could predict what his fares for the next week would be. But yes, when he was in a good mood, he was found selling the best biryani masala in the world. I was fond of Cornelia and I wanted to impress her with my culinary skills. So, I reached Ottakring in the morning on that day.

'Ask any shopkeeper for Hassan Pakistani,' I was advised.

He was easily found. One Sardarji had quite a hoard of Hindi film CDs. It was him that I asked right away.

'What a coincidence, Brother! Our Hassan Paa'ji is sitting right here!'

While we got acquainted, the old Sardarji was right beside us sitting with his stock of CDs, listening to us.

'So you belong to the hills?' He said to me even before I could speak, and I discerned an experienced voice with which he had started to interrogate me.

I was taken aback.

'How could you tell?' I gingerly asked.

'I would know a Kumauni mountain lad from Hindustan even in my sleep. Please tell me, what brings you here?'

'Ji, actually Rashid Bhai told me about you. He is my friend.'

'Then you must want the Biryani Masala of Hassan Pakistani.' He calmly said while slowly folding an open jacket, 'Rashid always sends his acquaintances to me for this. How is his daughter?'

Rashid, who worked at a pizza shop, had a daughter afflicted with polio since childhood. He had left his homeland and somehow reached Vienna with his daughter for her better upbringing.

'Ji, she is healthy. Goes to a school here at Ottakring. I think she's in fourth grade now,' I humbly answered.

'Hmmm.' He had started to contemplate something.

I watched him closely. He would be seventy-seventy-two or thereabouts. He had a tall, toned body with a wrinkled face, and on it there were a pair of moist, melancholy and bespectacled eyes. He also had a long, snowy beard. I was puzzled by his knowledge of my locality.

I had befriended many people from India and Pakistan. Among those I made friends with, there could be someone who knew us both. This person could have told him about me, I rationalized.

'You see, I don't have that spice readymade. When exactly would you be needing it?'

'I have invited some four-five friends over next Sunday. That's when I need it.'

'Not to worry. Let us...let us meet in the afternoon outside of Reddy Brother's Indian shop on Jumme-raat.'

How? I had never been to Reddy Brother's Indian shop. My face must have betrayed how clueless I was.

'Go straight up from here. After passing two blocks, from the third four-point crossing, turn right. A hundred steps from there, you will find a tiny church. Right in front of the church, there is a billboard for Western Union Money Transfer. That is Reddy Brother's shop. If I am not already there on the appointed day, please wait for me. Reddy knows me. He stocks one of the best Basmati rice. And oh, the spice powder will cost twelve euros.'

By then, Sardarji had opened a thermos brought from home and had already poured three cups of tea. Shyly, I took a cup.

Discerning my shyness, he said, 'We are all brothers here. That is how you survive in a foreign land. As it is, you are from our own community, Ji.' He placed a friendly hand on my shoulder.

On my way back I decided to take a look at Reddy's shop. It turned out to be quite a resourceful place. Apart from Basmati rice, I even grabbed my favourite beer brand from India, as well as some rare Pakistani CDs of Mehdi Hassan's ghazals.

Nevertheless, I still found myself wondering as to how the old Hassan Pakistani had recognized me as being from Kumaun. And I found that I longed to meet him again within such a short span.

On the said date, I was at the said shop. The old gentleman had not reached but Reddy recognized me swiftly. Reddy, from a small township of South Karnataka, had a degree in Civil Engineering. He had even bagged a job in Bangalore, but a yearning for the good life brought him to Vienna twenty years ago. While I was listening to his story, his wife arrived with a food-laden tiffin box. Upon her arrival, she asked, 'Hassan Bhai hasn't reached yet?'

Reddy introduced me to her. A Malayali, she was a nurse at a hospital. They had celebrated their twenty-fifth wedding anniversary only last month.

Reddy opened the bottles. We sipped on our beers and waited for Hassan Pakistani.

When the old man sheepishly entered the shop an hour and a half later, Reddy's wife scolded him lovingly and in mock protest, 'What, Hassan Bhai! You add to my chores. I cooked Paranthe and Malabari gosht for you. And you turn up now! It has all gone cold.'

The shop was closed for some time. We had lunch. Nobody even asked if I wanted to eat. A plate was straightaway handed to me. Between delicious food and beer, I quite forgot the purpose of my visit. It turned out that Mrs Reddy not only had great culinary skills but was a great conversationalist too. She managed a one-way conversation around the studies and career of her two children. She chatted us up the entire time, so it was not possible for me to talk to the old man about his personal life.

She kept on asking the old man's opinion on whether the couple should relocate to India after the children settled down with jobs. The old man slowly munched on his food and said to her philosophically, raising his eyes from the plateful of food, 'Wherever contentment lies!'

Then, he began to narrate elaborately the story of his family's journey from India to Austria. The hours slipped away and we didn't know when it was already five and the shop reopened as his tale continued. Outside, the streetlights came on and I looked at the watch. The old man had given me the packet of spices, in lieu of which I had paid. Thanking him from the core of my heart, I was just stepping out when I heard him say, 'Which way are you headed?'

I had a few books to return to the library by the Parliament. Not very far. I could have walked or taken the tram. I said so.

'I hope it is not inconvenient if I accompany you?'

I smiled and shrugged. I agreed when he suggested we walk. Thirty-thirty-five years of living there and he knew each road and by-road old and new, like the back of his hand. Instead of taking the main road, he took the dimly lit narrow streets of the Turkish living quarters.

In all my months of living in Vienna, I was treading such streets for the first time. I was beset with mixed emotions of apprehension and excitement. As we approached the end of that alley he asked me, 'Which ghazal of Mehdi Hassan do you like most?'

Taken aback a little with the mention of Ustaad's name, I answered, 'There are many but "Ye dhuaan sa kahan se uthta hai (Where does this smoke-like thing rise from)" is a favourite.'

'Hmmm,' he was lost in thoughts.

I was trailing quietly behind when something occurred to me. Finally, I risked the question, 'How did you immediately know me as a Pahadi the other day?' A little spooked, he looked straight at me and broke into a smile, 'Because I am a Pahadi and I am from the Almora town of your region.'

It was as if I fell from the skies. My own childhood was spent in Almora and I kept on frequenting it now and then.

'But you are from Pakistan...'

'Yes, I came away to Karachi in 1951.'

'Oh!'

'Have you heard of Liyaquat Ali Khan?'

The name did ring a bell, but that was about all.

'I knew you wouldn't. You couldn't have. He was like your Nehru Ji no, your Jawaharlal Nehru! Similarly with Pakistan. He was the first Prime Minister. Poor man was assassinated within a year.'

'Oh!' I felt that the old man was swapping topics because he did not want to talk about Almora.

'Won't you ask me why I mentioned Liyaquat Ali Khan?'

'I don't know. What do I say? It's beyond me,' I realized that I had a stammer. 'There! That is your library. You return the books while I order tea here.' We were in front of a Turkish tea-room from where the main road and library were clearly visible. Surprisingly, we had reached there in no time.

Upon returning, I found the old man puffing away and chatting with another person of his age, seated on one of the open tables in front of the tea-room. Black tea with milk-white palm candy arrived for me. The old man introduced us. It turned out that the other was the owner of the tea-room.

'Ismail Bhai's Abbajan arrived from Istanbul a century back. He is a close friend!'

Some half an hour passed in exchanging stories. Once again, we found ourselves in those narrow alleys after bidding goodbye to Ismail Bhai. I had the 48 to catch from Ottakring. I was yet to hear his own life story. He cleared his voice, 'So, as I was saying…' 'Ji.'

'Liyaquat Ali Khan, as he was called, was from Karnal in your Haryana but the lady, his wife, was from Almora, like you and me.'

'What are you saying, Hassan Bhai!' I exclaimed in astonishment.

'Of course, what else! If you went back five to seven generations, you will find common ancestors. She was from a true-blue Brahmin family of Almora, except that her father embraced Christianity but never gave over his caste. The good woman, Irene Pant was her name, poor soul. She taught in Delhi before partition, the story goes. That was where she met Liyaquat Sahib. Fell in love, got married. Pakistan was created. Liyaquat Ali became Wazir-e Azam, Prime Minister. Then he was shot by someone. His Begum, however, stayed back in Pakistan; she poured herself into philanthropic work so much that people started to call her Mother-of-the-Nation. About fifteen-twenty years back, she was recalled by Allah. That's about it.'

'This is weird. I had no inkling of all this!' I was astonished.

'You are not alone in not knowing. Political regimes do not allow people to know. They are the root of all this anarchy. By the way, we were neighbours with Irene Pant's family at the Hiradungri area of Almora. My Abbu was a travelling salesman for clothes in nearby villages. He had a penchant for music, so he became the Harmonium player at the local Ramlila. I lost count of how many times even we played the role of the monkeys, being youngsters, at the Ramlila. We kids would get laddus and samosas as remuneration.' The old man sat down on a roadside stone bench. He indicated to me to sit too. He was lost in his childhood memories. He fondly recollected the famous pahadi sweet shops of Almora and its old market. He would speak in stops and starts, then he would remember something and start again.

'I think it is time for your bus,' he made as if to rise in haste. I told him my 7:40 bus had long gone. The next was at 9:15.

'Oh, oh I apologize, Janaab. My monologue must have really tested your patience.' I put an arm around his shoulders, 'How can you say this, Hassan Bhai. Such great stuff you are telling me. As it is, I had no pressing need to be home. I would just have gone home and slept.'

'Then let's move a few blocks ahead. There is a park close to Reddy's shop. We may sit there. We can keep an eye on your bus stop that way.'

As we started to walk, I asked him, 'Hassan Bhai, you said you were from my place but did not say how you knew me?'

'No matter where one may go or what one may do, a genuine man is bound to carry his hearth, his village, in his dialect and intonation. The moment you opened your mouth to ask Sardarji over there about me, I understood that this man is Kumauni. That is all.'

It was autumn and a breeze had started to blow. Dry leaves were being tossed about in the air on the roads. I looked up at the sky. Nothing was visible beyond a thick layer of clouds.

My thoughts flowed all around the globe — Almora, Pakistan, Karnal, Karachi and a nameless empty alley in a European city. Then I thought of the old man. As far as I was concerned, I would go back to my own nation in a few days. This old man, huddled on a park bench, which nation would he go to? What is a nation after all?

To escape the maddening circle of my own thoughts, I took out my cigarette pack. I lit two, handed him one and asked, 'How did you reach Karachi from Almora?'

'Hmm.'

He took a long puff and started to speak. 'Irene Pant's uncle said one day that he would get his well-connected niece to recommend me for a good position somewhere in Pakistan. In any case, half of my family was already there after partition. My Abbu and Ammi had already passed away. So I pocketed a letter of commendation addressed to the Begum Sahiba of Liyaquat Khan Sahib, somehow arranged for the requisite documents, and reached Karachi the same fateful day on which someone in Company Bagh of Rawalpindi shot him dead.' He extinguished his smoke and put his hands in his blazer pocket. 'There was a curfew in the city and I was starving. The owner of a dhaba, a genial Chowdhury, fed me and gave me work in his dhaba. In his training, I learned to cook Biryani.'

'What about your family?' I couldn't wait. I wanted to know everything.

'Chowdhury lived alone. He had adopted me as a son and when he passed away twenty years later, I possessed two profitable dhabas, a wife and two daughters.

Things were running smoothly but Altaf's greed ruined everything.'

'Altaf?'

'My best, closest friend. One fine day, he ran away with my wife and daughters. He even usurped all my money. I searched for them a lot. Some say he took them to England, to Canada. Some also say that their car went over a mountain ridge on a road in Baluchistan and all the occupants died.'

'And then?'

'Nothing! It was not as if I had anything left. An agent took seven thousand rupees and brought me here. I passed my last thirty years sifting dust on these streets.'

The old man had fallen silent. The air hung heavy between us; so heavy that breathing became difficult. I looked at my watch. There was half an hour to my bus.

'So, where do you intend to go from here?' He asked after a short silence.

'Hmmm!' I said while reaching for my cigarette from my pocket, 'Next month, I will travel home. And then we have to see. I haven't made any plans yet.'

'It is good to have one's own home. Better still to have one's own nation. It is really great. Wherever one is, one should be happy!'

For a while, the two of us watched the leaves rolling about in the air on the field. The old man seemed lost. He started to hum the same ghazal sung by Mehdi Hassan,

'One whose moorings you have torn
How can he ever sit and rest?'

It was evident from his humming that he was no inexpert melodist. Then he stopped humming as well.

After a while, he asked, 'Do you know where Mehdi Hassan is from?'

'Should be from somewhere in Pakistan,' I pretended to be smart.

'Mehdi Hassan's house is in your Rajasthan. Village Luna, District Jhunjhunu. However, the poor man cannot travel there. It is all business. People are slaves to the regime.' Now, he even spilled out a thick expletive. Hassan Pakistani, Mehdi Hassan and me; our homes and nations were in the same place, but that night, all three of us were searching for a home and a nation.

Translated from the Hindi by Dr Mandira Chakraborty

A writer and translator, Ashok Pande lives in Haldwani, a small town in the foothills of the Kumaon Himalayas. He has published a poetry collection, a novel, an anthology of fiction and several travelogues. He has translated more than two dozens books of poetry and fiction from the world over.

Hearts and Minds

Ranjit Lal

When our new neighbours shifted in across the landing, I was eager to see if they had kids my age (I'm Rohit Sodhi, fourteen, aspiring cricketer, which is a hope in hell) I could be friends with. You see, due to a congenitally defective heart that was running out of steam rapidly, I'd had to drop out of school (even if home-tutoring is becoming an 'in' thing), and had spent the last two years at home, mostly alone as my parents were working. When this happens, your old school friends gradually forget you—and social media doesn't cut it with me at all; I tried it, of course—Facebook, Skype, and other 'chat groups', but I found them weird. I mean, everyone just gasses on and on about themselves and toots their own horns. Nobody else in the building we lived in had kids my age and going down to play cricket or football with the other kids in the neighbourhood was just out of the question for me. So—what the heck was I supposed to do with my free time? There is a limit to how much you can read or listen to music, or practise the piano or surf the net (which also got on my nerves because it felt like it was all make-believe and not real) or enviously watch the other kids run and scream and play. I wanted real flesh-and-blood friends with whom I could exchange high fives and slap backs and share wicked grins and crack dirty jokes. My parents didn't seem to notice this—I think they were just hugely grateful to God that I was merely alive and breathing.

Well then, the neighbours moved in and I knew something was wrong right away. Normally, Mama would have made something nice (brownies, a cake, muffins) and taken it over to welcome them, and called them over for a meal, but this time, she didn't. Also, Papa came home from work that evening in the car pool as usual, but looking like a thundercloud. Meanwhile, I had been sneaking looks out of the front door and the verandah all day, as I watched the moving trucks being unloaded and workmen bringing up stuff.

The new family consisted of two adults—a paunchy looking man with untidy hair and intense eyes, and his plump rosy-cheeked wife who smiled at everyone—and, last but not least, two girls in jeans and tees who looked like twins about my age. I took in my breath sharply: they were quite fair, pink-cheeked, and with light-green cat's eyes and dimples that showed when they smiled, which they too did to everyone, and silky brown ponytails which they swished around.

Papa works for this gigantic multinational that employs people from all around the world and we live in a block of flats owned by it. So, neighbours could be from anywhere in the world, which could be interesting, except that the ones that had just moved in were from, as Papa sourly put it, *'across the border!'* That meant we were to have nothing to do with them. You see, Dadaji, who had been a major-general in the army, had been paralysed waist down and had lost an eye due to enemy fire during the last war and Papa (who had been a smouldering sixteen-year-old at the time) had never forgiven the enemy for doing this, even if Dadaji had gotten used to his rakish eye patch and to racing around in his battery-powered wheelchair, and could joke raucously about them.

One evening, perchance we found ourselves in the lobby, waiting for the lift at the same time as the neighbours. We were on the tenth floor and I knew that neither family was going to wait while the other went up first. Sure enough, the lift doors sighed open and we all poured in: the two girls and their father followed by me and my parents. (The 'enemy' had been waiting longer than us, so got the first right of entry, I suppose.) This was the closest I had gotten to the sisters and they both really were stunning; they had lovely snub noses (with tiny emerald nose rings that matched their eyes), healthy pink cheeks, and lovely sylph-like figures. They smelt heavenly too, and when they smiled at each other, it kind of made you smile idiotically back at them. The adults completely ignored each other and that stainless steel lift felt icy as a coffin: no one said anything. Had they been from anywhere else, Mama would have been gushing over the girls and inviting them over by now, but she just stared at the floor indicators as the lift rose.

As for me—alas, by the time we had reached the fifth floor, I knew I was falling head over heels in love with both girls. I know, it seems weird and silly, and that they were the 'enemy', but when you're fourteen and have been in 'solitary' for as long as I have, these things happen. I did manage to sneak them a quirky grin, which they caught, and sent their shapely eyebrows shooting up into their foreheads.

By the time we had got home, I knew one thing: I had to find out everything I could about them. Well, I knew where their dad worked—and in what capacity—and the great God Google was extremely helpful.

Their dad's name was Syed Mohammed Arif Khan and he was reputed to be a wizard designer of medical robots which assisted surgeons in complicated operations, and other such complex equipment. His wife was a scholar of Persian and was into research. Wow! Even better, they had twin daughters: Jameela and Jasmeeta, but alas, although I scoured Facebook and Twitter and other social media platforms, they were obviously not on them. There was one thing I knew I just had to do: to establish some sort of contact with them, regardless of the consequences. So I hung out on the verandah every afternoon, waiting for their school bus to drop them, peering at them between the railings with my binoculars, feeling like a hideous peeping Tom, but what else could I do? Sure, they knew I lived next door, but did they know anything else about me? Surely some of the other kids in the neighbourhood would have told them about 'the sick freak on the tenth floor'? Once I saw them get down from their bus, I would go and stand near the front door and pop into the landing when I anticipated the lift's arrival with them and pretend I was going down. I would actually go down a couple of floors and then come up again!

After this had happened a few times, they caught on! They knew I was waiting for them: one day, they were both standing at the lift doors as I emerged after a brief foray to the fifth floor and back. They were standing, arms across their chests, side by side, smiling sunnily, tapping their feet. Ambush!

'Hi,' one of them said, 'I'm Jameela and that's my twin Jasmeeta. If Abba knew that you'd been spying on us, he'd really blow a gasket! So you'd better be careful!'

'I haven't...' I knew I was going bright red. 'Likewise,' I mumbled, 'Papa has an awful temper.'

They smiled again and lit up the whole landing. 'We don't mind: it's nice to have a secret admirer!' they giggled. And then, glancing at each other (they were pretty savvy chicks I tell you): 'Whom do you like better?'

I should have tried to answer them, because I never got another chance. I just fumbled and mumbled and went scarlet and grinned inanely. And then, a few days later (I think it had all become too much for my heart; the palpitations had started drumming madly again) I was back in Florence Nightingale Hospital, with blue lips and nails, breathing heavily and rapidly. The doctors looked grim. They said I needed a new heart and it could be a very, very long wait indeed. Exhausted and blue I lay back in my hospital bed, thinking of my dream girlfriends.

About a week later, Dr Abhilasha suddenly materialized at my bedside one evening and smiled at me.

'Rohit, we're getting you ready for surgery immediately—we found a new heart for you,' she told me, looking both sad and happy at the same time. 'It's young and healthy and its parameters match yours perfectly. You've been very lucky, son!' She paused: 'we have decided to try something different: we think your own heart is quite capable of functioning but needs a long rest. So we're going to piggyback the new heart to yours so it can take over and give your own heart some R&R!'

'Oh...oh, wow!' was all I could say and then; there was Mama and Papa to contend with as they turned up.

I was back home from the hospital within a month, but now Mama—and Ms Dee, the nurse who had been employed to look after me, hovered over me 24X7, ensuring I took all my medication, etc. I was escorted down every afternoon (yes, I had chosen the school bus time yet again) to walk up and down in the garden with Ms Dee as part of my rehabilitation. Well, the school bus came, every afternoon, but neither of the twins was ever on it. Oh crap—they'd been sent off to boarding school, I thought, wondering whom I could ask.

Then one Saturday afternoon, about a fortnight later, as I and Ms Dee waited for the lift again, a police jeep drove up. To my surprise a couple of burly cops emerged—they seemed quite senior—and got into the lift with me. I was dumbfounded when they too got off on the tenth floor with me (after looking at me up and down)—and then rang the bell of the Khans' flat.

Oh God, I thought, maybe Papa had been right to be so suspicious and hostile after all.

'You know, cops are raiding the neighbours,' I told my parents excitedly. 'They came up in the lift with me. Are they going to arrest them? Do they suspect them of being terrorists? Were they making bombs or something?'

'Don't be silly, Rohit! They must have reported a burglary or something,' Mama said. 'And anyway they're leaving at the end of next month—they've been transferred...' She sounded both evasive and relieved.

'Oh!' My heart sank. I would never see my beloveds again and we'd hardly exchanged a couple of words. It was just too bad and not fair. But before they went, I just had to make contact with them again....

That seemed easier said than done, because neither of the sisters seemed to be around. Till one afternoon, when I chanced to look out of the verandah and saw a blue Ford Figo draw up and park. Two people emerged: a lady with frizzy red hair whom I did not recognize, and one of the twins—I wouldn't know which! Well, if one twin was around the other couldn't be far behind I thought, suddenly exultant. To my surprise, they headed for the garden and sat down on one of the benches there, and began chatting. I looked around: Ha! Ms Dee was snoring on the divan. I sneaked out and went down and then hung around in the lobby as if waiting for someone (which I was!). Ten minutes later, the red-haired lady and the twin turned up. Quickly I undid the top two buttons of my shirt so my magnificent railway line scar was on display, and joined them, waiting for the lift.

'Uh, hello!' I mumbled as I followed them into the lift. Then I baulked. Jasmeeta—or Jameela—looked terribly pale and gaunt; her cheeks were sunken, she had lost weight, and there was no smile, just a silver glimmer in those lovely eyes. Had she been ill too? And where was her twin? To my shock, I felt her hand brush mine as she stood beside me, and for a moment, our fingers met and curled around each other. She squeezed my hand and I felt transported to heaven as I squeezed it back, our fingers properly entwined now. She glanced at me via the lift mirror and I think her pupils widened when she saw the top of my scar. The red-haired lady remained oblivious.

That evening, I waited eagerly for Papa to return from office: it was the beginning of the month and he would surely bring his glossy monthly office magazine home with him. And there would surely be a report of my successful heart surgery—it's not something that happens every day, especially to fourteen-year-old kids. A couple of staffers from the magazine had come to interview and photograph me after my return from hospital and no doubt, the report would be all goo-goo and ga-ga over how brave I'd been, blah-blah. Well, the twins next door would also read it… Like Dadaji, I'd be a hero! And I'd already been holding hands with one of them!

I took the magazine and scanned it eagerly. Yes, yes—there it was, with me looking heroic, wearing that expression that suggested I was in great pain (all bogus) but bearing up to it… Great!

Then, my eye fell on an item framed in black on the adjacent page. There was a photograph too: of the Khan family and a brief write-up, with the heading:

'*Tragic Loss*'

'The management and staff send heartfelt condolences to the Khan family on the terrible and tragic loss of their beloved daughter, Jameela, in a hit-and-run road accident. Jameela, just fourteen, had begun crossing the road when she was sideswiped by a car.'

Otherwise unscathed, the back of her head slammed the kerb as she fell, and she died on the spot. Her twin Jasmeeta was in shock and was being counselled. The report went on:

The company personnel also applauded the courage and sagacity of the Khans for donating Jameela's body to the Florence Nightingale Hospital so her organs could be harvested. Most of her vital organs have already been transplanted into grateful recipients.'

I looked at the date of the accident: it was the same day that I had got my piggyback heart....

I gulped. My mind raced: Would Papa and Mama also read the report and guess? And would Dadaji know, and how would he feel?

But most, most importantly, next door, would Jasmeeta also read both reports? And would she too come to the same conclusion?

That there was only one way she could get (and remain) close to her beloved twin sister for a long time to come?

Or had she already known? Was that why she had clutched my hand so hard in that cold stainless steel lift?

Ranjit Lal is the author of 45 books—fiction and non-fiction—for children and adults who are still children. His interest in natural history (particularly birds), social issues, automobiles, photography and cooking is often reflected in his work. He has won the Crossword Children's Book Award twice and has been honored by IBBY (2012) for his book on female infanticide, *Faces in the Water*.

Genes

Kausar Jamal

This tale is thirty-two years old, but even today, it remains green and fresh, like leaflets just sprouted from a seed.

The pleasant mid-September weather of Peking was tickling me with the thought that perhaps this time, I would be able to enjoy my freedom without a roommate. Most international students had already arrived in the first week of September itself and I doubted if any more students would come. But a call from the international students' office soon proved me wrong. My new roommate was arriving the next day, from Delhi, India. I faced this news with mixed emotions. A Chinese girl from my class had been my roommate for the last two years. We both studied the same discipline—Chinese literature. Because of this, I had benefitted greatly from her presence. My Mandarin had become quite fluent by speaking to her night and day. She used to go home for the weekends and her parents lived in Peking, and, even if just for a day, I used to find some freedom in my solitude. But the present situation was that there were fewer rooms in the hostels than the number of international students vying for them. So, now, we foreign students had to share our rooms with other international students.

Like I said, I faced this news with mixed emotions. I regretted that my freedom was now gone for sure. Neither would she go anywhere nor would I. And then, this habit was also common to us subcontinental students—instead of English or Chinese, we would rapidly slide into Hindi-Urdu. Speaking in our own tongue would be a source of joy that was always missing in a foreign tongue. I thought about the fabulous conversations that would ensue with the new roommate, even if my Mandarin fluency would get affected. But I also rejoiced thinking that I wouldn't have to hesitate while cooking anymore, as the strong smell of desi masalas would no longer upset my roommate. It's true that our cuisine is delicious, but its fragrance does not always please foreigners.

The next day after lunch, Prof. Chang brought her over. The previous day, I had cleaned her side of the room. Her side also had a single bed with bedding, a blanket, a duvet, an almirah, a book shelf, and a writing desk. The university had also provided all students with a thermos to carry boiling hot water. The responsibility for heaters and dishes to cook and eat in our rooms was ours.

'This is Komal from India, and this is Kausar from Pakistan,' the professor introduced us.

I surveyed Komal from head to toe. Fair complexion, big droopy eyes, plumpish, tall, clad in jeans and an Indian kurti, with a tilak on her forehead and sindoor in her hair parting. This meant that not only was she married but that she was exceedingly traditional too. The revelation that her roommate after coming abroad was a Pakistani was no less than an explosion for Komal. This much was evident from the incredulity on her face. I could understand her position because if two years ago I had been in her place, I would have felt exactly the same. First coming to a foreign country, and then getting a roommate from a country about which she would never have heard anything nice — all this was a lot for her to process. Even I had such mixed thoughts about my Indian friends in the beginning. But once mutual friendly relations grew, it did not take long to break down the feeble impressionistic walls of our minds; those impressions which get created in the minds of the youth of our nations about our neighbouring countries. On both sides, media and school textbooks always work towards agitating young minds over the Partition riots and the various wars between the two states. The moment there is any tension at the borders, there are zindabad and murdabad slogans thrown into the air, with equal intensity, on both sides.

'My dears, you people are such good friends, but then, why are there all these wars and demonstrations of hate in your countries?'—when our English friend Alfred said this, he had no idea of the kind of response he would get from us. Akash had immediately snapped: 'Why do you ask us, mate, you should know better about it.' Akash's words carried sarcasm tempered with a penchant for history, hearing which we had all guffawed together. But Alfred spoke again without understanding Akash's comment: 'Guys, you all are exactly the same, when you sit together, I can't even tell who is from which country!'

'Long live…,' and 'death to…' or 'down down.'

Mira and Akash from North India, Hasan and I from Pakistan, and Satish from Nepal, were part of our group in those days. We all spoke the same language, although our elders had given it different names. They had also left no stone unturned in trying to make their language different from the others. Upon hearing Alfred, I don't know how the following words came out of my mouth: 'Our genes are the same.' Everyone's jaw dropped open, and we clapped each other's hands in joy and guffawed together in delight at this notion. And Alfred got to hear many similar statements: 'We share a love-hate relationship.'

'You know, this is sibling rivalry.'

And so, my new Indian roommate was standing in front of me with her luggage right in the middle of our room. She was completely shocked and so troubled. I stepped forward, shook her hand and said: 'Kaisi ho, Komal, safar kaisa guzra?'

'How are you, Komal, how was your journey?'

'Oh, you speak Hindi!'

'Urdu, not Hindi.'

'Your Urdu is just like Hindi,' she said.

'Well, they were both really the same language, that Gandhi and Premchand called Hindustani. But no one listened to them,' I replied. Komal came out of her emotional turmoil upon listening to me. She now sat down comfortably on her bed. Professor Chang had left right after introducing us, but so far, we had been standing during our conversation.

Komal took some time to get used to her routine at the university and to settle into our shared room. I found her to be not very talkative. And not being talkative was quite an impediment to her Mandarin learning. She spoke to me in Hindi only, which I called Urdu. Our conversations would often bewilder her. One day she said: 'Please don't mind, but you don't seem Pakistani at all!'

'I am Pakistani, just quite a liberal-minded, progressive one. I love all humanity. And Pakistan is not devoid of such people at all.'

She looked at me as if it were difficult for her to believe me. I continued, 'Actually, I don't seem Pakistani to you because the conception of Pakistanis in your mind is quite different. Two years ago, even I was like you, I too had only a superficial understanding of Indians. But my experiences proved my conceptions to be wrong.' I bent towards her and whispered secretively: 'We have the same DNA.'

Sheer wonder was evident on her face. But I went on speaking: 'See your colour and mine, our tongue and its flavours, our dress, our way of life, our attachment to our land—is there any difference at all? Our ancestors have lived together for centuries in this land, their civilization cannot die in half a century.'

'But our religion is different,' she pointed to the one difference between us. Such a blood-sucking difference that it had divided a centuries-old country and coloured its boundaries with the blood of millions of humans. 'We can have a long conversation on this, Komal. It is a matter of evolution. The history of religion is not older than that of a few thousand years, but the DNA I am talking about is far older than that.'

Most of our conversations like this one took place at night, before we dozed off to sleep. The conversation thread was picked up every night, right where it was dropped the previous one. One night, she asked me a lot of questions about Islam, which proved to me that she knew next to nothing about the religion. Two years back, I was also like this with regard to Hinduism. But in the last two years, I had studied all the major religions of the world. Not only had my reading enhanced my understanding of the spiritual world of humans, it had also strengthened my emotional makeup. When I told Komal about the ethics and directives of Islam then she promptly responded: 'Arey, we have very similar notions in our dharma as well.' Over time, the unfamiliarity between us waned. We were both similar in possessing sensitive and affectionate souls. The topic of our conversations now turned towards our pasts and our family members. I told her that my father had not given me permission to study in China. In fact, he had got offended forever with me, because, according to our family traditions, a single woman was not expected to go abroad for her studies. And this was despite the fact that I had received a scholarship for my studies.

I tried really hard to convince him but he did not agree. Abbaji had disowned me on this issue, but the rest of my family stood by me. I had grown intensely despondent thinking of the rift dividing my father and me, but… what do you know, Komal had started weeping!

Actually, Komal had remembered her own grief. Komal had married for love two years ago. The boy was from a different caste. Her family had broken all contact with her over this. She had started crying thinking of the night when a few months after her wedding, her father had passed away because of a heart attack. She had gone home tremulously for one final glimpse of her Pitaji.

'Kausar Ji,' she told me interrupting herself with long sobs, 'my heart begins to bleed even today when I remember that night. It was the first time that I realized that I had become a stranger to them forever. Some of the women of the family slyly connected even Pitaji's heart attack to my marriage. My mother, sister, brother—no one was willing to hug me and share my grief.'

Komal went on talking between her sobs. Her grief had found its way out. That night, I hugged and comforted Komal affectionately. I wiped away her tears and made her tea. It is said that we come ever closer to those with whom we share our pain. This is what transpired between Komal and I. Earlier, she would lock up her cupboard and keep her plates and dishes separate from mine as she was a vegetarian. But now, her cupboard was freed from the padlock and our crockery became one. Nonetheless, I was always careful never to cook any meat in the room. One of us would cook dal and sabzi, and both of us would eat it together. I would sometimes go to the hostel dining hall to eat my favourite food.

Time moves at a strange pace during the years of university study in a foreign country. Sometimes, days of leisure are impossible to get through, with loneliness and the memories of home. At other times, such as under the pressure of studies or during exam days, time flies away on wings. And so, we completed my third and Komal's first year at the university. I was here for four years to receive a degree, while Komal had arrived only for two years to learn Chinese and collect material for her PhD dissertation. She was to go back and write up her thesis on the spread of Buddhism in China. I was also to go back and write my PhD dissertation and I had chosen my topic. I had decided to undertake a comparative study of the works of the greatest modern Chinese litterateur Lu Xun and the tallest of the giants of Hindi-Urdu fiction writing, Premchand. When I told Komal about my topic, once again she posed a question full of innocence: 'Kausar ji, have you read Premchand?'

'Yes, of course. Premchand's books are part of our syllabi.'

'But he wrote in Hindi, and you can't read it.'

I told her that Premchand was more of an Urdu writer than a Hindi one. He had first started writing in Urdu itself. It was only later when the Hindi publishing market improved and got bigger than the Urdu market that he moved to writing in Hindi. But all of his books are available in Urdu too.

But with Komal's intervention, I thought about learning Hindi, since I knew that some of the criticism published on Premchand's work since his demise was not available in Urdu. The very next day, I met the head of the Hindi department so that I could seek his guidance to learn Hindi. He made an interesting point: 'You don't need to learn Hindi, but only the Hindi script. There is hardly any difference between spoken Hindi and Urdu. Albeit, quite a bit of difference has crept in between written Hindi and Urdu over time. Consequently, you might need a dictionary to read Hindi books.' That night, I was sitting in my bed with a Hindi primer. Komal glanced at it and started laughing.

'Arey, Kausar ji, you should have told me if you wished to learn the Hindi script. I would teach you in a way that you would never forget it.' Komal was right. She taught me the Hindi script in a way that I have never been able to forget it. Even today, when I close my eyes, I can vividly remember the pages of the notebook where, every morning, Komal would write some letters in the first line for me to practice emulating on the rest of the page. Everything was going smoothly between us so far. But I don't know what happened suddenly, some bitterness arose and that created a distance between us. I don't remember at all what the source of this bitterness was. Undoubtedly, it would have been one of the incessant border or political conflicts between the two countries. We must have argued about it, and it would have been blown out of proportion. Most definitely, there are certain such unresolved issues between our two countries that we must walk a tightrope to discuss. A little carelessness, and we common people move from picking the flowers of friendship and love to hurting ourselves on the thorns of misunderstandings. The amazing thing is that I retain all the lovely memories I built with Komal, but for the life of me, I cannot remember that one thing which became the reason for the extreme tensions between us. The intensity of our bitterness was such that we did not speak to each other for many days. When she would come to the room, I would go out, and when I would enter, she would leave. Many days passed like this. I even forgot to open the notebook I had purchased to learn the Hindi alphabet.

Then one day, Komal initiated a conversation: 'It's OK if you don't wish to talk to me, I am also not overtly keen to talk to you, but...'

When she paused at 'but,' I kept looking at her agape, wondering what she would say next.

'But... please continue to learn the Hindi script.'

'What do you care if I learn Hindi or not. When someone teaches me, I will learn,' I also retorted in kind.

But now, she was smiling.

'Open your notebook and see, I never stopped doing my side of the work, it's you only who has put in none.'

I immediately opened the notebook like a child. She was correct. Every day since our argument, she had written down a few new letters on a new page. But this time, she had not just written down the Hindi letters, but on each page, she had also written an English sentence: 'For the sake of our common genes.'

This was the moment when Komal truly won my heart. I looked at her with an embarrassed smile. She snorted with mirth and soon, we were both laughing together.

Translated from the Urdu by Maaz Bin Bilal, Delhi, India

Kausar Jamal is a writer and a linguist. She holds a Master's in Urdu literature and a PhD in Comparative Literature. She has to her credit six published books of research, translation and short stories. She has resided in Australia for the last 20 years and works as a freelance linguist.

The Ghost

Sehyr Mirza

The village residents had assembled in the courtyard in the swirling mist of the early dawn. The massive peepal branches enveloped the courtyard in an eerie shade. The glistening mustard fields, encircled by clusters of low-roofed brick houses, painted the monotonous landscape of the deserted village in hues of yellow and green. A herd of goats, sheep and buffaloes was grazing on the lush pastures near a water trough. Children hopped about on an old red rusty tractor parked under a shelter.

But the daily customary village routine was thwarted. The peasants hadn't taken their ploughs to till the fields. The women, clad in loose-fitted shalwar kamiz with chadars pulled over their heads, appeared petrified as they mumbled to one another.

Yusuf Baba, the village head, looked stupefied, seated on a wooden slab bench. The frail-looking elderly man, dressed in a beige-coloured dhoti-kurta, restlessly ran his fingers through the scanty hair on his head. 'I sighted the same ghost last night. We need to beware. Our village is possessed,' he urged.

The villagers gathered close to him as he spoke about tossing and turning in bed all night after he felt he had seen a ghostly figure.

'At half-past four, my sleep was interrupted by the faint buzzing sounds of pesky mosquitoes. I found thick layers of smoke frothing into my room, which gave me a whooping cough.'

'I quickly got out of bed to rush towards the window and caught sight of a mysterious figure of mist roaming a few miles over the fields, in the deep darkness of the night,' the villagers noticed Yusuf Baba's feeble hands trembling like a leaf.

A sinking feeling of paralysing fear swept over the crowd. The children jumped off the tractor and stepped closer. Their eyes were wide open as they hung onto his words.

'Plunging my head out of the window, I was shocked to see that the ghostly mist had turned into a hulking full-bodied ghost that disappeared into the air on the other side,' he recounted.

Cries of horror were heard from the crowd that had been anxiously hooked to Yusuf Baba's stories while recalling their own experiences of the ghost's presence in the village. Gossip was heard from all corners about uncanny happenings. Residents claimed to have witnessed strange marks on mirrors, some had heard heavy appalling voices, some reported disappearing items from their homes and some talked about doors being locked on their own.

A tall, full-figured woman in her fifties began beating her chest, screaming: 'This ghost is turning our village into a living hell, but whose ghost is it? It must be the ghost of the peasant who committed suicide last year.'

A short-statured herdsman standing near the peepal closely examined it. He scraped off a tiny piece of bark, ratifying that the tree seemed to be haunted. 'My forefathers were nomadic shepherds and I have heard from them that strange cracks in the tree trunk are suggestive of it being possessed by a female ghost,' he asserted, assuredly. 'I think it is the ghost of the bride who was killed on her wedding day a few years ago,' he added.

'No, there is something quite different about this ghost.... I exactly remember that ghoulish ugliness on its face....it is not from among us,' Yusuf Baba interrupted.

'Does it really come from...?' someone tried asking.

Yusuf Baba immediately completed his sentence in a guarded whisper 'I have told you many times that it comes from the other side. It is a Hindu ghost.'

A terrified woman dragged her five-year-old son into the middle of the courtyard, warning him against playing under the peepal tree till late in the evening.

'That ferocious Hindu ghost will eat you up if you don't come home earlier,' she commanded.

Hashim, a quaint young man clad in khaki trousers and a baggy navy-blue cotton shirt had been quietly listening to the crowd's snivelling. Considered a hopeless dreamer, he had a long-standing liaison with unemployment. He was either seen wandering aimlessly in the village streets or hatching bizarre schemes to flee from working in the fields. And was, hence, demoted to belittling status by the villagers.

'The Hindu ghost is all in your imagination. I have never seen any ghost in our village,' he stuttered, though, he suspected an outrageous response.

The villagers glanced at each other, tossing their heads in utter dismay as if they were convinced Hashim was possessed by the Hindu ghost. Yusuf Baba felt infuriated at being ridiculed thus despite for his accomplished age-old wisdom and sense of prophecies.

He jumped off his seat, clearing his throat rather loudly before he stated, 'The Hindu ghost is putting our lives in danger and you don't believe it. You want us to keep sitting on our hands?'

Hashim continued playing the ghost's advocate. An argument broke out among the residents.

Meanwhile, Yusuf Baba's gaze penetrated into the fields on the eastern side, where he would often see the ghost disappearing.

An extended high-iron fence surmounted by loops of sharp barbed wire obstructed the fields. A four-kilometre muddy patch—that belonged to no one—lay ahead, enclosed by another similar high-iron fence.

The sun was, by now, loitering above the horizon, brightly illuminating the enormous panoramic fine green verdure that extended a few miles down the village on the eastern side.

Some women carrying earthenware pots were heading towards the well to draw water. Some washermen were hanging laundry on the clotheslines surrounding a nearby dhobhi-ghat while others thrashed clothes against a stone slab.

A coral-coloured saree covered with spices, drying under the sun, was spread on the sloppy courtyard floor near a water pump. Ratna Devi, an ordinary-looking middle-aged woman, was seated on a charpoy, applying a home-made herbal balm on her bruised left foot. Another woman collecting dried spices for pickle enquired about Ratna's foot.

'I was coming downstairs from the rooftop yesterday when I felt like I was pushed by an invisible force. I lost balance and fell down, injuring my foot,' she disclosed in a low, pain-stricken voice.

The frightening expressions on the other woman's face could tell that her heart might be running a marathon. 'This matter is getting serious now. Do you know something similar happened with Bhavna, a few weeks ago?' she asserted.

'Did she also get pushed by the creepy ghost? May God keep us safe from this ghost's curse,' Ratna responded.

'I have heard she had been hearing some horrifying whispers and recently she also saw some words randomly appearing on her room's window, which she thought resembled Urdu,' the other woman said.

'What? Does that mean it really is a Muslim ghost?' questioned Ratna.

The village elder, Mohan Chacha, a cranky big-bellied man, was smoking a hookah while resting in a white metal chair. Overhearing the conversation, he spoke up in a rather irritable tone: 'We have been sighting the ghost for a while now, so we must be vigilant. But you should first go to see the doctor?'

'I could barely walk, but Chandar has gone to get a prescription from the doctor for me,' replied Ratna as she waited for her son's return.

Chandar seemed exhaustingly frazzled when he arrived after a hasty stride down the village centre. He came with the news that the clinic had been shut since early morning. For the past two nights, the doctor had been hearing someone slamming and forcing open his door. He had been perplexed and had fallen sick.

'I am coming straight from the village centre and people just can't stop prattling away for hours about that ferocious Muslim ghost,' claimed Chandar.

Mohan Chacha sucked in a deep breath, appearing nervous by the turn of events. Suspecting danger, he called in for all the villagers to assemble outside his house to decide their most suitable course of action. The peasants were called back from the fields. The village women suspended their household chores in the middle of the day—and everyone gathered outside Mohan Chacha's dilapidated single-roof house.

People were closely huddled together. The sounds of a heated debate started reverberating as residents plunged headfast into their stories of encountering the Muslim ghost. Everybody frantically waited for their turn for a catharsis while recalling their dreaded memories of the ghost.

A man claimed to have seen some mysterious footsteps around the border area. Another warned that the winds appeared ravenous closer to the border, as if they would blow one off their feet. Someone believed that the wrathful Muslim ghost was bloodthirsty and it intended to bring them harm. After chewing the cud for about a few hours, the residents arrived at a consensus that most people had seen the ghost toiling around the barbed wires.

'We have enough evidence that the vengeful Muslim ghost will cross back to its own side whenever someone catches its sight,' said Mohan Chacha.

'And it is now in our best interest that we call upon Swamiji Dharam Raj to pay us a visit and ward off the Muslim ghost, once and for all,' he continued.

The residents nodded their approval to Mohan Chacha's advice. Also present in the crowd was the goat-keeper, Akash, a 22-year-old clean-shaven man who had his dull brown muffler wrapped around his head in the form of a turban. He whispered to Chandar, seated next to him, 'Let's go near the border area tonight to spot the Muslim ghost before it is gone.'

Chandar was shell-shocked. He instantly turned down the idea, though he was somewhat tempted to answer in the affirmative.

'We can't put ourselves in such a danger…it's not an ordinary ghost…. it's a vengeful Muslim ghost.' he asserted, as his eyes cautiously wandered around.

'Imagine our heroic return after confronting a Muslim ghost that has shaken the entire village. We will be considered the most daring people in the village.' bragged Akash. 'Sakshi will also be impressed,' he laughed. His face flashed with a sense of pride as he revelled in his approaching achievement.

Closer to midnight, the heavy yellow moon was shining on the face of the dark star-strewn skies. Both Akash and Chandar showed up near the village's tube well. Akash had wrapped a khaadi shawl and was carrying his long sturdy stick. Chandar's hunchback became more visible as his half-bent body turned stiffer and colder with fear. Tightly holding a lantern in his left hand, he walked with Akash as they took to the dreary path etched between the fields.

They reached close to the barbed wire in nearly twenty minutes. They stood there stealthily; their gaze remained frozen to the other side to catch that one glimpse of the Muslim ghost crossing into their side.

'I have heard from my grandmother that ghosts don't reveal themselves to everyone,' Chandar uttered timidly, as if he had already surrendered, 'So, it might not appear tonight and we might as well go back.'

'Half of our village has seen that Muslim ghost and so will we. Don't try to chicken out at the very last moment like a coward,' responded Akash.

He wasn't finished yet when they heard some creepy high-pitched screams echoing in the night air. The screams seemed distant, but their exact source was not identifiable. Chandar squeezed his eyes shut, turned back and in a flash of a second started rushing back through the same rugged path that had brought them there. Akash's display of utmost bravery had almost vanished. He could feel his emotions tumbling and body quivering as he ran back unsteadily after Chandar. Akash tried to persuade himself that they hadn't heard any screams, though deep down, they both seemed convinced that the Muslim ghost was chasing them.

'Akash, run faster. And don't turn back,' said Chandar. Defeated by his flaring fit of curiosity, Akash, however, did turn back. He found no one behind. But noticed some fidgeting in the houses across the border. He saw lights in some of the houses gradually switching on.

Hashim, lying on his shabby charpoy, also heard the scream. He staggered down from the rooftop through a crumbling staircase and overheard an ongoing conversation about the Hindu ghost's screams from a house in the neighbourhood.

The next morning hadn't only brought with it an agonizing sense of fright but had plunged the village into spirals of lamentation. Shahid, the short-statured herdsman, was mourning the loss of one of his cows—his very source of income.

'It had not even occurred to us in our dreams that the Hindu ghost would make our cow disappear,' murmured Shahid's wife as tears filled up her eyes. Two other village women snuggled close to her, holding her tightly in a comforting embrace.

Yusuf Baba offered his consolation and informed them that the Peer Baba Yaqoob Din was on his way. 'He will be here anytime soon and will destroy the Hindu ghost, you just wait and see,' Yusuf Baba's tone got grim and furious.

Shahid, seated at the edge of a rumbled chair as his legs paced restlessly, said, 'Peer Baba is the only one who can capture that spiteful Hindu Ghost, but don't you think that the police should also be informed?'

Hashim cautiously interrupted, 'I also heard the deadly scream last night. I am quite convinced it is the Hindu ghost. Why in the world would the Hindu ghost trust us beef-eaters with a cow?'

The villagers mocked him despite his ultimate acceptance of the Hindu ghost. In the eyes of the villagers, he was a deranged man who made conscious efforts to provoke. While Hashim made preparations to leave for the city, the Peer Baba arrived.

The old man was rather tall and strong for his age. His face was luminously bright and a prayer bump was visible between his thick eyebrows, bearing testimony to his piety and religious devotion. Draped in a crisp white shalwar kurta, he donned a skullcap that partially covered his thick grey hair.

The Peer Baba received a courteous standing ovation from the village residents. Men came touching his knees to pay him respect. A finely decorated blue-coloured sofa, considered the best in the village, was brought from Yusuf Baba's house for him to sit on. A splendid meal was laid out for him on a lustrous dastarkhwan. Not much time was lost in his pompous bragging about triumphantly hunting down ghosts before he began his exorcism rituals.

'I have acquired the knowledge of capturing ghosts from our forefathers. We have been serving people for decades,' he revealed.

He displayed a set of items on a wooden table beside him; his bag exhibited several distinct herbs, spices and bottles of oils that were each prepared for use against different kinds of ghosts. He pulled out and burned some exotic leaves, placing them inside an intricately carved metal plate.

Soon, the air got heavier with the smell of burning leaves. Inhaling the fumes, he began chanting and synchronically spun his head at a tremendous speed. Having fallen into supposedly a mystical trance, he spoke another language.

He revealed in his steady, raspy voice that he had an encounter with the ghost. 'This ghost has all the sinister qualities possessed by the Hindu ghosts,' he confirmed.

'It is not just ghoulish to look at but can prove to be fatally threatening for the village residents if not expelled soon,' he commanded. His face assumed an ambiguous smile, revealing warning cues to the villagers, 'Some ghosts are easier to hunt down, but this infidel Hindu ghost might require several sessions.'

A startled child in the courtyard inquisitively asked his mother, 'Amma, do we have to feel more scared when a ghost is a Hindu?' 'Yes, son, our own ghosts are innocent, god-fearing beings. Hindu ghosts are infidels and can go to any extent to cause us harm,' explained the mother. The stunned look on the face of the child meant he'd been scarred for life.

Having half-heartedly witnessed the torturous exorcist rituals, Hashim finally set off on his journey to the city. He drifted down the village streets reminding himself of his plan for the day: he was going to pick up the hidden cow from the abandoned dirt ground, occupied by the craggy families of nomads, and then head straight to the main avenue leading to the city to sell it.

'Now that the Hindu ghost was responsible for the cow's disappearance, why must he feel guilty and tolerate the callousness of the villagers,' he thought to himself.

He, however, seemed puzzled thinking of last night's deadly screams that Akash was also still reeling from.

Akash was trying to rise from beneath the comfort of his quilt in the middle of the afternoon. The Muslim ghost's scream gave him nausea-inducing goosebumps whenever it replayed in his ears.

Still dazed by slumber, he washed his face with the water drawn from the hand pump in the courtyard. He heard Mohan Chacha's irritated voice from behind, 'You could also have sought Swamiji's blessings had you gotten up a bit earlier.'

'Swamiji was here? Did he catch the Muslim ghost,' Akash asked.

'Yes, he almost captured the Muslim ghost but it's not so simple. Organized poojas, which Swamiji will be leading, will be held in the village on specified dates, and the Muslim ghost will ultimately be cast off to where it belongs,' responded chacha.

'Swamiji informed us that this Muslim ghost has devoured many Hindus. The repulsive-looking ghost is cannibalistic and will continue its terror on our land until it is expelled,' added chacha.

Ratna Devi, leaning against the wall near her doorstep, breathed out a deep sigh before saying, 'I have been asking Chandar to recite Hanuman Chalisa but he never listened to me. Last night, he got tremors from a high fever.'

'Yes, Chandar is possessed by the Muslim ghost. Swamiji could even see the Muslim ghost hiding behind his blood-red eyes,' disclosed chacha.

'The Muslim ghost still hasn't left his body and the fear is that if it stays longer, my son might start speaking Arabic,' cried Ratna.

Akash didn't utter a word. He sat down on an elevated stone slab in a head-down position with his legs wide open and hands clasped in the front. Guilt trickled through him as he raised his head and glared at the remotely visible barbed wire in the fields. Recalling last night's ordeal, he was engrossed in deep thought.

How could the fields tremble with the whooping sounds of the screams? Why were the winds so wrathful there? How could the screams engulf the entire area in their firm grip? He broke into a cold sweat as he tried to dig deeper into the mystery. He stared at the abandoned four-kilometre piece of land between the two villages.

'That patch of land that belonged to no-one, might it, in fact, belong to someone?' he thought.

'No, but why would it then target us Hindus only?' he quickly refuted himself.

The ghostly screams continued to echo in both villages, getting all the more alarming and fearful. Uncanny happenings in both the villages didn't come to a halt. Strange footprints were captured, items were moved and disappeared, mysterious whispers were heard, petrifying shadows emerged from the fields and residents were randomly grabbed and pushed.

The fear in the villages continued to heighten. The two villages appointed their own guards to defend themselves from the menace of the ghost. Security vans were also seen patrolling to catch anything out of the ordinary at nights. But the ghost didn't leave.

The villages sank into a deeper state of distress and panic. Many startled peasants stopped taking their tractors to the fields. An eerie silence prevailed in the deserted village streets. The fields of gold steadily turned into a desolate wasteland. The sickly bodies of the children soon became crooked as their limbs shrunk. The dark circles under the eyes grew deeper on the pale, haggard-looking faces of the villagers.

Special prayers led by Peer Baba and Swamiji continued to be held. But the ghost still didn't leave.

As days turned into weeks and weeks into months, the accounts of the ghostly presence reached adjoining villages and from there, they spread deeper into smaller towns and several big cities. And that's how, gradually, the fear of the ghost became larger than the ghost itself.

Sehyr Mirza is a creative writer and journalist based in Lahore. Her work has appeared in leading media outlets such as Deustche Welle, BBC, Himal Southasian, Outlook India, The News on Sunday, Dawn and The Huffington Post. Her practice encompasses narratives that navigate the themes of memory, shared histories, loss and nostalgia. She holds a degree in English Literature from Goldsmiths, University of London.

Going Back

Anushka Ravishankar

Pydhonie, Dongri, Agripada, Gamdevi, V.P.Road, Byculla, Bhoiwada, Nagpada, Kherwadi, Nehru Nagar, Dharavi, Ghatkopar, Kurla, Deonar, Trombay, Bandra, Vakola Jogeshwari.

It's a strange feeling, coming back to Bombay (it's Mumbai now, but it was Bombay then, and I can't come *back* to a place I was never in). I don't remember much along the way when we ride from the airport to Andheri, but when I reach Lallubhai Park, my first feeling is, god, nothing has changed. The buildings even seem to have the same paint that they had all those years ago. There's a sadder feel to it all, though. Everything looks dirtier, less hopeful. The way I remember it, it was happy and bright. But then, I was eight, and happy to be playing with my cousin in the stairwell and the garden.

I'm impatient to go to Lokhandwala Complex, to the old flat. We set off in an auto. I grin at the familiar landmarks on the way (though there are many things that my mother points out that I have no memory of), and feel mildly betrayed by the changes and absences. The autowala charges an amount that seems ridiculously low to us, used as we are to the bandit autos of Chennai. My mother speaks to him in Marathi. He replies in Hindi, impatient.

We reach Apna Ghar Society. It's an unreal moment. The park is still there, but it looks small and dry and terribly pathetic. For some reason, it reminds me of my mother's old aunt, balding and sad and abandoned by everyone. The buildings are the same, but they're a different colour now, and the windows look unfamiliar.

Having got this far, I'm ready to turn back. I don't want to meet the old neighbours; I remember them only vaguely and feel unprepared for the 'How much she's grown!' 'She was so tiny!' 'She looks the same!' 'She looks so different!' that was bound to follow. Why can't they think of other things to say? Like, 'Did you know that the chameleon can move its eyes in two directions at the same time?' or 'I just discovered that Sherlock Holmes never said "Elementary, my dear Watson."' At least one can have a conversation about these things. Instead, I have to smile and mumble and laugh inanely.

Someone should write a book which will teach people some original and interesting things to say when they meet young people whom they haven't met since they were babies. Maybe I'll do it. Children can gift the book to all their relatives and family friends. At least they won't have to go through this ordeal when they grow up.

Unfortunately, my mother is unimpressed by my speech. We go to house after house; she rediscovers affections that had obviously been dormant all these years. I'm amazed by her! For god's sake, she hasn't thought of some of these people for seven years, let alone spoken to them. Looking at her, one would imagine that she had been bosom friends with all these aunties. While in fact, she only met them in the park, where she sat in the evenings to keep an eye on me and my friends as we played. I tell her this between houses, and she denies it.

'I used to visit them,' she claims. 'We were neighbours; these bonds are hard to explain. Didn't you enjoy meeting Sneha?'

I did not. We ring another doorbell.

My old friends have grown into aliens. Could I have made mud-pies with this supercilious girl? Could this boy with the carefully parted hair be the little brat who insisted on coming to see me the moment he woke up every morning? Before he even brushed his teeth (eeuw!)! What is a person, I wonder. A collection of bone and tissue, an occupier of space? I often think about these things. I've always assumed that the person I call 'myself' is a collection of my memories. But those memories suddenly seem unimportant and distant now; as unreal as a dream. So then, what becomes of that 'I'?

Suddenly, I'm jolted out of my thoughts. I'm aware of a sudden silence. Had someone said something to me? Were they waiting for me to answer? I look around in panic, but no one is looking at me. There's a crackle in the air. I'm good at recognizing crackles. It's a skill that comes from living with a mother who can embarrass one to death by telling one's super-dignified school principal that she likes his socks, or going to a meat shop owned by a Muslim and asking for pork. It is the same kind of crackle. It's the same fall in temperature that follows soon after it.

My mother gets up to go. There's no more hugging. Obviously, something has happened, and I, as usual, have missed it completely. We leave in an auto. I want to walk down Lokhandwala street, eat pav-bhaji at the corner shop, if it is still there (odd how clearly I can remember the look and taste of that pav bhaji), peer into the barber shop where I was shaven bald, meet the grocer who always gave me a lollipop when my mother went to buy provisions at his store ... but I know better than to try and penetrate the black cloud that hangs over my mother's brow.

Suddenly, I notice that instead of going back to Lallubhai Park, we're going in the opposite direction. We come to a new building. It's not a place I remember. We get out, go in, and ring a bell. A woman opens the door.

'Meenakshi?' my mother asks.

She stares at my mother for a moment. Then she looks at me and her eyes widen. There is a gasp in her breath as she says my name.

My mother smiles her relief.

'I'm sorry,' she says. 'We should have kept in touch. We should have called to find out how things were with you. But you know how it is. One gets caught up...'

'It's alright, it's alright.' She is clutching my mother's hand now.

'I can't believe they did that, I can't believe it,' my mother's eyes are filling up.

'They did what they had to. People feel insecure.'

'You should have sued them. You have as much right to live there as they do.' My mother is working herself up into a fury. I begin to get nervous.

'Let it go. I have,' the woman says, but I'm not sure I believe her, because there's a burden in her voice. 'This place is better,' she says, and I don't believe her at all. Her voice is too thin to carry the weight.

But my mother is beginning to get calmer, and I breathe easier. A different dread is building up, though, somewhere at the back of my head, and I don't even try to go there. There's a memory hidden there, I know, and I'd rather not find it.

'I wonder if she'll remember you,' says the woman, smiling at me. 'Wait.'

I don't want to wait, I want to leave, but of course, there's no question of doing that.

The woman goes inside and comes out leading a girl. She is so beautiful! She always was. The first time I saw her, wearing a blue frilly frock, with her thumb in her mouth, she looked like a fairy from my storybook. But later, I found that she talked very little and didn't play with the other children. She took a great liking to me, though, and every evening in the park she came and stood near me, watching me play and holding my hand whenever she could. I hated it. The children in the park didn't want to play with her, so I didn't either.

But if I pushed her away, I had to deal with my mother's scolding, and worse still, with a look in the girl's eyes that I only recognized much later, when I saw a boy pull a dog's tail. So, I bore with it, as much as I could.

'She's not my friend,' I told all the others who teased me because of her, 'She's not! She's not!' I was only eight.

My mother would not understand.

'They're insensitive, stupid children,' she said. 'You don't have to be like them.'

Still, I had my own ways of rejecting the girl. Secret ways that only she and I knew of. Though it's difficult to be sure if she knew anything. She still followed me about the park, and came home with her mother so she could watch me read or draw. She never tried to join me in what I was doing. She just looked. Sometimes I got irritated, but sometimes, it didn't matter. I'd put a dab of paint on her nose, and laugh at her. She'd look back at me and I sometimes thought I saw a smile in her eyes. But I could be mistaken.

She was not my friend, she was not.

When the trouble began, I didn't really know. It was only slowly that I realized that something horrible was going on in the city.

Pydhonie, Dongri, Agripada ...

My mother wept every time she watched the news. When I asked her what happened, she told me about a mosque that had been broken down, about how the Muslims had reacted, and how the Hindus had reacted to the Muslims' reaction.

Gamdevi, V.P.Road, Byculla, Bhoiwada, Nagpada ...

I suddenly learned about us and them. We were not Muslims. The Muslims were them. So, did that mean that the people who were doing bad things to Muslims were us? That didn't seem right.

Kherwadi, Nehru Nagar, Dharavi, Ghatkopar...

My father did not go to his office for a few days. He went part of the way one day, and came back looking like he'd seen a ghost.

'What is it? What is it?' my mother asked, but he would only shake his head.

Kurla, Deonar, Trombay, Bandra, Vakola, Jogeshwari ...

'It's alright, it's safe here,' my parents kept saying to each other.

We were allowed to go to the park, but only if there was an adult with us. Sneha's mother was keeping an eye on us that day, but she had to go in for a minute because there was a phone call.

'Don't go out of the gate, I'll be back in a moment,' she called.

We were too busy playing to bother.

Suddenly, there was a man at the gate. He was talking to the watchman in a loud voice.

'Don't tell us there's no one here! We have information! You don't need to do anything, just tell us the flat number.'

'Let's ask the children,' said another man who was with him.

So they came towards us.

'Is there a Lakdawala in this building?' they asked.

We looked at them. We had been told not to talk to strangers, but these two men looked alright, so we didn't move away. Suddenly, one of them saw her. She was standing just behind me, clutching at my skirt in that irritating manner she had.

'Look at that one. What's your name?' they asked her. She looked at them dumbly.

'What's your name?' one of them asked again.

'Anjum,' said a boy.

One of the men took a step towards her. I don't know what it was—maybe it was the look on his face, maybe it was the things I'd seen on TV, and the things I'd heard my parents say, but suddenly, I stepped back and hugged her.

'She's my friend!' I said, and looked into the man's eyes.

For a moment, we stared at each other, the man and I. The other man moved forward.

'What are you waiting for? Didn't you hear that? Her name is Anjum.'

'No, it's not,' said the man I was staring at. 'You heard wrong. It's Anju.' He turned and looked at his companion.

There was a moment of silence, and then my mother came with Anjum's mother and Sneha's mother. They were all shouting. The men turned and left. Everyone seemed to be talking at the same time. I couldn't hear a word they were saying, because I was crying. They had to pry Anjum away from me.

Soon after that, my father got a transfer out of Bombay, and I rarely thought of Anjum in all those years. She was not my friend.

I stand up.

'Anjum,' I say and go towards her. On a sudden impulse—where did it come from?—

I hold out out my hand. She looks at me, and there's not even the hint of a smile in her eyes. She has forgotten me completely. I feel like a hole is opening up somewhere inside me. If you disappear from someone's memory, does a part of you vanish?

I try to smile at her, but my lips refuse to listen to me.

'We should go,' my mother says. 'I'll keep in touch, Meenakshi,' she promises.

'It's Mumtaz now,' says Anjum's mother.

'You converted? But you always said ...'

'I changed my mind.'

She smiles, but there's something in her eyes that looks like a lost world.

Anushka Ravishankar has written several books for children and young adults, including picture books, chapter books and rewritten folktales. Her latest book is *Ogd*, a book that is profoundly nonsensical, much like the world these days.

Christ's Statuette

Mubashar Aziz Hassan

Amid a posh locality of the city, there was a deprived neighbourhood of Christians, also home to a few Muslim families. Mohammad Hussein's abode was among the few Muslim homes in Paras Town. The humble man Mohammad Hussein ran a sort of junk shop. He always tried his utmost to help those in need, even beyond his means. Content with whatever he was bestowed, he was much respected in his area by all and sundry due to his humble nature and piety. He had been living in the area along with his wife and their only son, ten-year-old Ahmed, for a long time. Ahmed was in class five, and Mohammad Hussein wanted him to acquire higher education to achieve new heights. It was because of the efforts of Pastor Barkat Masih that Paras was an exemplary town where they all lived together peacefully.

Respected by everyone, Pastor Barkat was a pious and genial man. People would seek his advice to settle their internal and external issues, and his judgement was always acceptable to both parties. He lived in people's hearts and strictly believed in the doctrine of non-violence. He talked to people affectionately, with a bent-down head and in a low tone. It was his inner positivity that reflected on his calm face. He had two daughters, Maryam and Sonya, who were quite young, and a son, Youhana, who was also the classmate and best friend of Ahmed, Mohammad Hussein's son. They shared a strange bond and their friendship was exemplary.

Pastor Barkat was cautious about the education of his children and wanted them to benefit from the teachings of Jesus Christ to the fullest. He knew that the only way to live in this mortal world was through piety and that it costs nothing to be kind towards fellow beings.

Mohammad Hussein always fulfilled the wishes of his son generously, and never turned them down.

One day, he brought home a sack full of used, imported toys from the flea market for his son. And when he untied and emptied it on the floor, Ahmed was overwhelmed with mixed feelings of happiness and surprise.

'This is all yours, my son,' he said, with a glowing face of a father upon seeing his child happy. Rather, he was happier than his son.

Looking at the heap of toys, Ahmed's mother objected, 'Why did you bring so many toys?'

'Our son is happy and that's enough' Mohammad Hussein replied calmly.

Ahmed forgot about the evening meal and kept sorting the cars from the other toys. Then, he turned to the soldiers that were in abundance in the heap. Some of the soldiers were crawling with their guns while the others were charging, brandishing their guns. A military truck, a crane, a big golden fish, and a helicopter whose rotors were broken, were also lying in the heap. Most of the toys had parts missing but Ahmed didn't notice this anomaly in his excitement. Most of the toys depicted military action, making Ahmed feel as if he possessed an invincible military might.

Ahmed was very excited to find a fancy black horse, which he wriggled in the air holding it from its tail.

There was a pair of wolves, which were holding up their snouts as if howling, along with a donkey with a saddle. There weren't any tigers, cheetahs, giraffes, monkeys and elephants in the toys, but whatever was there, was more than enough to play with and explore for months.

Before leaving the house, Mohammad Hussein was immensely pleased to see his son rifling through his toys.

After having inspected all the toys, Ahmed was surprised to find a small statuette under the sack. The statuette was of a holy figure he had seen at Youhana's home, but he wasn't aware who he was.

The beauty of the statuette could not be expressed in words—a dove sitting on a shoulder and an arm raised in the air. The statuette had all the characteristics that could enthral anyone.

Winter was still afar, and the quilts hadn't yet been brought out of the zinc trunks. Thinking for a while, Ahmed went upstairs to the storeroom. He opened the lid of the trunk, climbed into it and placed the statuette beneath a bundle of rags under the quilts.

After arranging all his cars on the parapet of the house, Ahmed asked his mother for the canister in which rice was stocked. She reluctantly handed it to him after moving the rice to a different storage box. Ahmed placed all his toys in the canister and put a small lock on it.

After sunset, the rooftops and the alleys of this poor neighbourhood were submerged in darkness. Dilapidated roads full of muck, irregular tiny abodes, hanging electric wires, and ghostly human beings who would kidnap any child passing by under their shawls and strangle them to death after raping them—all this was not uncommon in this poor neighbourhood.

There was nothing but poverty, desolation and oblivion outside Mohammad Hussein's tiny house. Fall was about to end and the gloomy days of winter were just around the corner.

Ahmed thought that had his father not forbidden him from going out at night, he would have gone to invite Youhana over to see his toys and they would be playing together. Children are usually possessive about their toys, but theirs was an ideal friendship, and even if Youhana had asked him to give him the entire treasure of toys, he would have surely given in.

The next day, Ahmed's mother laid a floor mat in their tiny courtyard for both boys to play with the toys. Both crouched on the mat and examined the toys, starting with the cars. Ahmed felt a renewed surge of happiness sharing the toys with his best friend.

Ahmed said to Youhana, 'Let's start a battle. You take half the soldiers and I take the rest. You take the helicopter and I take the tank.' They placed an oil-stained pillow between the two forces to mark the border and started an India-Pakistan war. 'You are India and I am Pakistan,' Ahmed said, to which Youhana replied, 'No, I am Pakistan and you are India.' Ahmed was so enthusiastic about his new toys that he would also have agreed on becoming Israel. A furious battle ensued, with the boys making horrible sounds with their mouths. The helicopters were gunned down and the tanks were crossing the border made of the pillow, and both the sides were trying their best with their military acumen and tactics to overcome the enemy. They were in the middle of their battle when they heard someone calling Youhana's name from the drawing-room.

'Youhana, O Youhana,'

'Yes, mom, what is it?'

'Your dad is calling you upstairs, hurry'

'OK mom, just coming'

'No, go right away and see what's your father saying. Come again afterwards'

Youhana got up reluctantly and said to Ahmed, 'I'll just come back. Then we'll start it over again.' When Youhana was gone, Ahmed gathered all the scattered soldiers, military hardware, and animals and put them back in the canister.

December had just begun and the quilts were to be sunned a couple of weeks before the season. Ahmed checked the statuette under the bail of rags in the trunk and went back to his room on the ground floor.

It was just another listless winter noon, when Ahmed went to Youhana's home. A large painting of the Christ, hanging on the wall of the sitting area, captured Ahmed's attention. He kept on staring at the painting for so long that Youhana asked, 'What are you looking at?' 'Nothing,' Ahmed replied promptly. Ahmed had seen this portrait so many times at Youhana's home but never asked whose painting it was. On Ahmed's curiosity, Youhana replied, 'That's our Lord, Jesus Christ.' 'What if I give you a beautiful statuette of Christ?' Ahmed again asked. With religious fervour, Youhana replied very courteously, 'I'd be more than happy, dear.' Youhana knew that gifts and presents cement a friendship. He had learnt the noble virtue of gratitude from his father.

'And if you give me that statuette on Christmas Day, it would be a double treat,' Youhana suggested. 'I'll tell my father and mother that Ahmed presented this to me, and they would be happy too.' 'How did you get this statuette?' Youhana asked, to which Ahmed just kept silent, lest Youhana's happiness wither away.

'Come, let's play outside,' Ahmed said ignoring Youhana's question, and they both went out to play in the street.

On 20 December, one of Mohammad Hussein's nephews died in a road accident and they all went to Sahiwal for the funeral. Before leaving, Ahmed went upstairs to the storeroom, fetched the statuette from the trunk and put it in the canister with the other toys. When they got back to Lahore on the morning of 25 December, the first thing Ahmed wanted to do was to gift the statuette to Youhana. Ahmed wanted to wrap it in colourful gift paper, the same way his maternal aunt had gifted him a sweater. But it was a national holiday and the shops were closed, so he took out a fancy piece of crimson fabric from his mother's cupboard to wrap around the statuette. When he opened the canister, the statuette wasn't there. 'How can it be,' he muttered. He looked inside the canister once again and then went upstairs to check the trunk, but it wasn't there either. He went back down and emptied the entire canister on the floor, but the statuette wasn't there. It was already noon and Youhana would have returned home after the morning Christmas service, he thought, and headed straight to Youhana's home. Standing by the window, called out his name, 'Youhana, Youhana!' to which Youhana asked him to come in.

It was a bright but warm day for late December. The Christmas tree was fully illuminated. The light, in different colours, was shining through the multi-coloured windowpanes of the house.

Youhana's mother promptly brought the pudding made of granulated wheat, which was specially prepared for the occasion, garnished with almonds and pistachios. Ahmed had two platefuls and then turned to Youhana. 'You remember I wanted to give the Christ's statuette to you on Christmas?' 'Yes, I remember, dear,' Youhana replied. 'Well, it has gone missing...' Ahmed's words pierced through his ears like a hand grenade.

'Gone missing? What do you mean by gone missing?' 'You didn't have any statuette, you lied to me,' Youhana burst out in anger.

'No, I am not telling any lies, I promise,' Ahmed explained.

Youhana didn't want to have an argument as he had to go see his aunt Mrs Robert with his parents, so Ahmed got up silently and left broken-hearted.

In this entire neighbourhood, Ahmed had no other friend or even a cousin to seek consolation from, so he had to patch up with Youhana by any means and make him believe that he wasn't lying. When he went again in the evening to see Youhana, the latter seemed cold.

Youhana wore a new attire, more attractive and dandier than the one he had been wearing in the morning. It was an immaculately stitched three-piece suit, with a necktie. A strong fragrance was emanating from the coat. Sonya and Maryam were also clad in glittering attire and held their purses, which they would open and close every few minutes and then hang again over their shoulders.

'Why did you lie to me?' Youhana asked disappointedly, 'You know, God hates lies. You must not do that to anyone.'

'I didn't lie to you,' Ahmed responded emotionally.

Youhana was upset as he wished to present Ahmed to his parents as a well-mannered boy, so that they wouldn't object to their friendship. Although Youhana's parents already thought of Ahmed as a nice guy, without bringing in their difference of faiths, the statuette, by all means, was still important.

Pastor Barkat was also home when he heard a faint gist of what was going on. He asked the boys to follow him to their private prayer room. Ahmed had never been to this room before. There was nothing much in the room, except a green wall-to-wall carpet, an easy chair, and a bookshelf where some sacred scriptures were placed.

There was also a painting of Jesus Christ covered in blood hanging on the wall. It was in a different pose from the statuette in which Jesus Christ was on a cross, with a thorny crown on his head and hands nailed to the cross.

Two candles were burning in a candle-stand under the painting. The fragrance of the incense had enveloped the room. A strange calm and spiritual bliss could be felt in the air.

Both the boys stood quietly in front of Pastor Barkat, who had immediately sensed that all was not well between them.

'What happened, my children?' he asked, 'Ahmed, you tell me….'

'There was a statuette of Jesus Christ that my father brought for me, with some toys. I wanted to gift it to Youahana on Christmas but when I came back from Sahiwal, I could not find it. I looked carefully many times, but that statuette of Christ with a dove had just vanished somehow….' Ahmed ranted.

'What, what did you just say?' asked Pastor Barkat.

'The statuette with a dove… yes, a dove was there on Christ's shoulder, and his other hand was raised towards the sky. I also asked my father and mother, but they didn't know anything about it.'

Pastor Barkat had been in a state of religious fervour since the morning, which was gradually pushing him into the past. The surface of the river Jordan appeared calm, but the flow was so fierce that it drifted Pastor Barkat along. When he re-emerged from the water, a strange sight was awaiting him.

'*…as soon as Jesus was baptized, he went up out of the water. At that moment heaven was opened, and he saw the Spirit of God descending like a dove and alighting on him. And a voice from heaven said, "This is my Son, whom I love; with him I am well pleased."*'

As Ahmed narrated the story, his voice choked and he was about to burst into tears, Pastor Barkat affectionately said as he embraced and kissed him:

'Sometimes, when you wish to appease someone with a gift, you have to face certain ordeals. I am very pleased with you, my son! Children are the reflection of God. Their mistakes are ignored by Him. Jesus had called a little child to him and said: "Truly, I tell you, unless you change and become like little children, you will never enter the kingdom of heaven. Therefore, whoever takes the lowly position of this child is the greatest in the kingdom of heaven. And whoever welcomes one such child in my name welcomes me."'

'But Youhana says I am a liar,' Ahmed broke down in tears.

'Youhana, O he's crazy… Youhana, come here my son,' Pastor Barkat probed, 'What happened to you? Why are you misbehaving with your brother and being unjust to him? Have you forgotten the teachings of our Lord Jesus?' All the sacred verses that he had delivered in his sermon earlier in the morning were subconsciously coming back to him.

'Jesus taught us,' he said, 'if you love those who love you, what's the big deal in that, because even sinners do the same. If you do good to those who do good to you, how can you claim God's mercy, because even wrong-doers reciprocate in such a way? Do to others what you want them to do to you. If you highlight others' flaws, yours will be highlighted too. Don't blame others, otherwise you'll be blamed too. You will be forgiven if you forgive others. Love those who hate you.'

'Jesus told us to seek abundance for those who curse you. Pray for those who disgrace you. Love your enemy. Give whatever you have. Give away the shirt you are wearing if someone asks for it.

This is the rightful message that Jesus brought to us. You must keep it in the purest chamber of your heart.

Today is a blessed day. Bless yourself and bless others by spreading the message of our Lord Jesus,' he continued elaborating.

Ahmed was staring blankly at the burning candles. Youhana also seemed to have had enough of this. They both wanted to go outside and play with the sparkle sticks that Pastor Barkat had specially brought for Youhana. He had promised Ahmed months ago that they would play with them on Christmas Day, followed by the clay lamps whose wicks were placed on them very tactfully.

Both the boys were waiting impatiently for the sermon to end so that they could go outside and play. But Pastor Barkat's words were flowing from his mouth like a freshwater stream. It is written in the Holy Bible about His people:

'My sheep hear my voice, and I know them, and they follow me'

Maryam and Sonya were also seeing all that was happening, standing at the entrance of the room, holding each other's hands. They also sensed it was anything but normal today. Little Sonya was holding the Santa upside down by his feet.

Pastor Barkat asked the boys to hug each other. They kept on holding each other's hands for long. They knew it was time to go. They both waited for Pastor Barkat's final words to them, telling them to renew the bond of their friendship. They hoped that the resentment would fizzle out and they both would go out and play.

Pastor Barkat once again muttered, 'For the society that gives up on the virtues of honesty and harmony, the likes of donkeys, guns and wolves are sure to overpower it. May God help us spread love, peace, and sincerity to each other, Amen.'

He then made the sign of the cross and blessed them.

Translated from the Urdu by Bina Biswas

Mubashar Aziz Hassan is an Urdu fiction writer and literary academic from Lahore. His first collection of short stories, *Andhay Ka Roznamcha*, was critically acclaimed for its synthesis of social and psychological realism.

Shanti of Guru Mandir

Amra Alam

It is quite rare for someone living in Karachi to not have heard of Guru Mandir. The Guru Mandir Bus Stop is among the most crowded places in the city. Many families have been living there for decades. Only a few have moved in from other neighbouring areas. As the city expanded with the continuing urban sprawl, many people moved to new localities. However, there were still many who chose to stay in the familiar areas. Shanti Verma was one such person. Her small, two-room house stood like a dusty but well-loved memory in one of the dilapidated streets of Guru Mandir. Her husband had passed away decades ago and her children left one after the other to settle down in Dubai and America. Shanti Verma was left alone. But it was the love of the neighbours that never made her feel lonesome.

Everyone treated her like family, except a few people. Among them were Munshi Ram Lal and Ibrat Khan. Munshi Ram objected to Shanti Verma's closeness to people of other faiths. Ibrat Khan, on the other hand, disliked not just her but everyone from other faiths. His hatred was such that he could have barred them from visiting his shop.

Shanti, however, lived her life in peace, detached from enmities and hatred. There was an old crumbling temple down the street near her house. Shanti would visit the temple in the evenings. She would wipe the dust off the windows before closing them, clean the floors, and switch on the lights in the meditation hall. Visiting the temple and cleaning its floors and courtyard had become her daily ritual—a vigil she observed daily before retiring for the night.

In the courtyard of the old temple was a hand pump. Every morning, Shahid, Shyam, and Minni would meet each other in the courtyard as they filled their buckets with water. They would carry the buckets back to their houses before setting off to school.

The three of them were quite young but had never fallen victim to hatred against each other. Minni went to church every Sunday with her parents while Shyam would pray at the temple with his family. Shahid's father took him to the mosque every Friday and the boy also dedicatedly prayed five times a day at home. Despite several riots in the city, their friendship remained intact. They never let their religions intervene in their friendships.

It was winter. Everyone had been stuck in their homes since the evening due to a heavy rainstorm. Shanti was not feeling well. But despite the torturing pain that coursed through her back, she pulled herself up for her daily duty. What must be done must be done! And so, she dragged herself to the temple. She wiped the dust off the windows. The temple floors were covered with mud and debris. She picked up a broom and did what could be done. By the time she reached the central hall, the pain in her back became unbearable. Holding her back, she lay down on the temple floor and gradually fell asleep. Perhaps she had caught a fever.

The next morning, the sun returned, and the weather was seemingly pleasant. Shyam, Shahid, and Minni made their way to the temple courtyard with their buckets. They had an off from school and there was no need to rush back home. The three friends filled their buckets with water and then stayed a while to play hide-and-seek. Minni hid behind one of the pillars and noticed that the lights in the central hall were on. She stood there, wondering if she could turn off the lights without revealing herself. But she was shocked to notice Shanti's body lying there on the floor.

'Aunty Shanti!' she screamed. Quickly, Shyam and Shahid ran to her side. Trembling, she pointed towards the hall. 'L-l-look! Aunty Sh-Sh-Shanti has died!' Shocked, Shyam and Shahid looked up. Seeing the old woman lying there, they rushed towards the hall. Shahid touched her forehead and found it burning with fever. He looked at Shyam, who went out to fetch water. They dripped the water into her mouth. Minni, meanwhile, had also come in. She no longer looked frightened and rested Shanti's head in her lap. She massaged her temples and prayed for her to wake up.

Shanti opened her eyes. The three kids cried out with joy. 'Oh, goodie!' one of them said. Shahid ran out to the neighbouring shop to get some tea and medicines. Shanti, meanwhile, had sat up, feeling much better from the care she had received.

A crowd had gathered outside and curious onlookers peered into the central hall. Among them was Munshi Ram Lal, screaming angrily at the old woman.

'O, Shanti! How dare you allow a Muslim in this temple? And you even drank his tea? Shame on you! It would have been better if you had died instead!'

Ibrat Khan, hearing his Hindu rival, responded. 'Die? How could she die? Witches like her do not die! They don't have the luxury to die! Look at her! Leading that Muslim child astray!'

Shanti got up and walked out. Looking at the two men, she said, 'Munshi Ji, Khan sahib, why do you say such horrible things? Do not scare these poor children! Tell me, does religion forbid us from helping the sick? And Munshi Ji, if taking medicine and water from a loving friend makes me a sinner, what is the point of such a fragile faith?'

Turning around, she placed her hands on Shahid and Shyam's heads. 'Today, these kids cared for me so lovingly. Had my own kids been here, I doubt they'd have done the same! Why should I push them away? Why should I discriminate between them? And you tell me to do something so horrible?'

Shanti would not stop. The people listened to her, spellbound. But when she turned around to face the crowd, she saw that Munshi Ram Lal and Ibrat Khan had left. Minni, Shyam, and Shahid stood by her, as if protecting her from the crowd. The people started to leave, and Shanti sat down by one of the temple walls. The three children resumed their game. Everything seemed to be fine.

Unfortunately, people who seek to do evil can't be turned down so easily. Ibrat Khan and Munshi Ram Lal were two such people. They may have run away from the crowd but they were teaching the people to hate. They were filling their hearts with a poison that would slowly destroy the neighbourhood. Wherever they bumped into each other, they would immediately start cursing and calling names. They would give speeches against people from other religions. They would spread rumours, make up stories, and turn friends into foes. Their hate speeches were so convincing that ordinary people would be driven toward them. Hence, their poison spread like wildfire, and Guru Mandir started to change. The small and narrow streets were now filled with conspiracies.

In those days, Guru Mandir was home to a number of Hindu families, many more, in fact, than those who live there now. For decades, they had lived there peacefully with other religious communities. Religion, for them, had never been a cause of strife. The people were friends, and they would never think about ruining their friendship over differences of creed. On Eid, when the Muslims celebrated by sharing sweets, they did not care if someone was Hindu or Muslim. All that mattered was that they were friends. Similarly, when the Hindus celebrated their Diwali, they would also share sweets with everyone, regardless of their beliefs. After all, sweets are sweets! They are not Hindu or Muslim. So, why differentiate?

Most of the educated people believed in harmony, but because of the daily conflicts, they also turned bitter. Friendships were crumbling, and it seemed like Ibrat Khan and Munshi Ram Lal had worsened the mutual differences between the neighbours. Their poison had reached the houses of the three children. Minni, Shahid, and Shyam were still friends, but their parents had been caught in the trap.

Shahid's parents had told him never to bring water from the temple again. They had also been forbidden to play together. But Shahid and Shyam did not give up. Shyam would sometimes sneak out at night and climb up to his friend's room. Hearing him, Shahid would rush inside to open his window, and the two friends would spend the night talking and playing games. If no one else could be seen nearby, the two would call Minni and the three of them would spend time together.

Shanti, meanwhile, was gradually growing old. Her stories were abandoned. The neighbours and their kids no longer spent time with her. Guru Mandir was turning into a place of turmoil. The conspiracies of the adults were impacting the children in the neighbourhood. They were afraid and would keep their distance from Shanti. Shanti was now left alone.

On a sad day when Shanti was preparing to take her morning bath, she heard a series of gunshots. 'Guns?' she asked herself, 'But why? Who is being shot? Who was shooting? What is going on?' What Shanti did know, however, was that these were the people from the neighbourhood who had lived like friends earlier.

Frightened, Shanti ran outside to see what was happening. 'Why are you doing this?' she wanted to scream. You were all friends a few days ago? There is no reason to fight! Tears welled up in her eyes and her vision turned blurry. When guns are shot, the bullets do not care whether a person is a Hindu or Muslim. They just kill. As Shanti ran out of her house, a bullet struck her in the stomach and she fell down.

Silence penetrated the streets of Guru Mandir after sunset. But the hospital was now home to sobs and groans. Shanti, too, was there, lying in a bed, bleeding from her wounds. She could not remember what had happened or how she was brought there. Outside the operation theatre, she could hear the murmur of people waiting for their injured relatives.

The doctor had pulled the bullet out from Shanti's stomach. But the immense loss of blood was making her faint. 'Do you have any relatives whom we can ask for blood?' Shanti was asked in a partially conscious state. Shanti thought about her kids. Her face was downcast with grief, and she was once again on the verge of losing consciousness.

The rising sun shone dimly on her face. The night had passed. When and how, she did not know. A nurse woke her, gently shaking her arm. The painful look on her face was fading. Her face looked a bit more alive. As Shanti opened her eyes, she saw Shahid standing at the foot of her bed. He was smiling. His mother was standing beside him, holding his hand,

'Nothing to worry about, ma'am,' the nurse said to her gently. 'Your blood matches perfectly with Shahid's mother, so you'll be fine.'

Shanti stared at Shahid and his mother. Their smiles slowly warmed her heart until tears of happiness welled up in her eyes.

Shanti's condition was improving gradually. She was not allowed to go home yet, so Shahid and his parents visited her daily. They would bring food and often sit down to eat with her. Sometimes, Shyam and Minni would join them and the old friendships started to revive once again. The clouds of hatred had passed and the storm of anger had ended. The sun shone again on those old streets.

One day, when they were all having lunch together, Shanti spotted a young man walking in from outside. He was neatly dressed and as he came close to her, Shanti smiled. Her face lit up. It was her son. After all those years, he had finally come to see her! The young man hugged his mother and told her that he had heard about the Guru Mandir riots.

'I am worried about you,' he said, 'and I have come to take you with me.'

She laughed when her son asked her to leave and said, 'What are you saying, my son? How could I leave? I belong here! You want to take me away from my home and my people? No, I will not go, I will live and die where I am! I will not leave!'

Shanti turned toward Shahid and his family.

'We are now blood relatives,' she said. 'How can I leave them? So what if some people fought? If some of them were killing, others saved me by giving their blood!'

Staring at her quietly, her son's eyes were wide open in astonishment.

Guru Mandir was turning into a happy place once again. Children could be seen playing in the streets. Munshi Ram Lal and Ibrat Khan's hateful tactics had no place in Guru Mandir anymore. They must not have given up on spreading hate but had moved away. No one knew where they had gone.

And so, time passed. The children were now adults, and the adults had now grown old. Shanti was now even older and weaker. Her friends and neighbours still cared for her, so she was never left to feel alone. Her house was small and dusty, with only two rooms, but her doors were open for everyone.

Everyone residing in Guru Mandir knew about Shanti. Be it the tea stall owner or the fruit vendor, everyone adored Shanti and offered her help in difficult times.

Gradually, the Muslim population took over the neighbourhood of Guru Mandir.

Most of the Hindus, Sikhs, and Christians had left to settle in other parts of the world. Shanti was the only Hindu left behind in the neighbourhood, but she was not alone. Shyam and his parents had also left for Dubai, but Shahid was still here and would always visit Shanti with his parents.

It was an autumn evening in the year 1990. Shanti was lying in her bed, staring at the roof. Shahid, now a college student, would visit Shanti on his way back. When he touched her forehead, he found that Shanti had a fever.

But as Shahid stood up to call a doctor, Shanti grabbed his hand to stop him. 'I do not need a doctor,' she said. 'The person I need is right here beside me.' Shahid looked at her, frightened, but she would not let him go. 'Look in my cupboard,' she said. 'Inside, you will find some papers and a wooden box. Bring them to me.' Shahid stared at her old eyes and nodded. He slowly opened the cupboard and brought what she had asked for.

Shanti looked at Shahid for a moment and then placed the papers in his lap. 'Shahid dear, I give this house to you. Sell it and use that money to further your education. And yes, get an education that teaches you to love. The world needs love, not hate.'

She then handed him the box, and said, 'In this box, I have jewels that I had kept for my daughter-in-law. When you get married, give these to your wife as a gift from your aunty Shanti.'

Shahid sat there, confused. He was not sure what to do. He wanted to get up, and to call for help, but Shanti held his hand tightly and would not let him go. Shanti's grip loosened, her eyes closed, and her breath became faint. The silence in the room was filled only with the faint sounds of Shahid's sobs.

Translated from the Urdu by Muhammad Munhib Shah

Amra Alam is a celebrated author of over 80 books for children. Her story book *Jhakkad* has been published in 12 different languages in the Indian subcontinent. Amra received the Anita Ghulamali Award for Best Story from UNESCO and ITA in 2014. Along with her story writing Amra has penned a number of popular theatre and TV plays.

Tears from the River

Saaz Agarwal

One of the things I remember most about my childhood in Sindh is our river, the mighty Sindhu. My brother Lal and I would sit by the window as our train crossed the railway bridge to take us home to Hyderabad from Karachi, and look down into the water. People would be tossing akkho, offerings of rice and other things, into the river to feed the fish and keep the evil eye away. And our elder brother Kanna would get off at the Kotri station to buy Kotri jo pallo.

Pallo is a freshwater fish, and it was a supreme delicacy in our home. Pallo is also a very bony fish, but they are soft bones, and if we tried to remove them as we ate, our mother would shake her head lovingly and instruct us, 'Chew! Chew!' because that is the way pallo is eaten.

When I was thirteen, we went to live in Bombay, and after that, our mother never cooked pallo in our home. It was a real treat for us on rare occasions, sometimes in our masi's home, but our mother would never eat any, and it made her cry when it was served. We children would see the other women flocking around to comfort her, hugging and stroking her back and saying 'Na, Devi, na!' We would feel uneasy and try to pretend that nothing was wrong and sometimes Lal would get angry and shout at Moti, our younger brother.

In Bombay, there was nowhere to run outside and play, as our homes were in buildings on the side of roads which had constant traffic on them. But when we lived in Hyderabad, Kanna and his friends flew kites in the lane outside our home or on the terrace. On hot summer evenings, he and his friends would dive into the Phuleli from the bridge, a fall of nearly twenty feet. They would practise swimming diagonally across the canal against the current, and the younger boys would watch admiringly, longing for the time when they would be able to jump in and do so as well.

In our families, girls were sent to school and treated with respect. My brothers were expected to do the hard work and, when people came to stay, they would be the ones who would have to carry their bags, and give up their beds and sleep on mattresses on the floor. We played marbles and ditti dakar with our friends and sometimes when Kanna was flying a kite, he would hand me the string so that I too could feel it soar in the wind. There would be competitions and the older boys would coat their strings with powdered glass to cut their rivals' kites down. And all of us marvelled at Dwarko's toys.

Dwarko and his family, whom we referred to as 'Javawaro', lived near our home, and he and Lal were good friends. Dwarko's father lived in Jakarta, where he ran a business. Dwarko had a lot of expensive clothes, and his home was filled with beautiful objects, including a small Japanese projector his father had brought for him on one of his visits home. I remember the excitement with which we would go to visit when he invited us to watch a Tom and Jerry cartoon film. When I was a child, moving pictures with vivid animation and loud music were a rare and special experience, glamorous and exciting! Dwarko had one reel with just one film, and we thoroughly enjoyed watching it over and over again.

Hyderabad had quite a few families like Dwarko's, whose fathers and elder brothers lived and worked in other countries, coming to spend a few months with their families every two or three years. Their large and beautiful homes had carved wooden furniture and marble floors, and some even had flush toilets, which were a great luxury since most of us had toilets which were cleaned by a sweeper woman every morning. Dwarko was an only child and he was used to always getting what he wanted, but he remained a kind person. We were fond of him and also awed by the fact that, when he turned sixteen in a few years, he would go to join his father in Jakarta and take his place in the family business.

Between our home and Dwarko's was a building in which Lila lived. She was one of six beautiful sisters and was the most beautiful, kind, and gentle of them all. I had the feeling that Kanna was in love with her and I would have been so happy for her to come and live in our home as his wife!

On the other side of our home lived Pesumal. He was the youngest of seven, and his mother had died when he was just a few days old, so some of the gossips tried to give him the reputation of someone whose very existence had brought tragedy to the family. Pesu was cared for by his grandmother, Ammi, and his elder sister Duru. Duru had requested their father not to remarry, promising him that she would care for all her siblings. To do this, she refused many offers of marriage which would have taken her into the lap of luxury. In the end, when she did marry, it was to Narayan, one of the sons of Judge Gehimal, a young lawyer educated in England. She was looked after so well that they even welcomed five-year-old Pesu to live with the family.

Pesumal's father, Lilaram, had been so broken by the death of his wife that he had lost his job in Lahore and come back to Hyderabad to live in the family home. He was Ammi's only son, but Ammi had also reared Santdas and Lokumal, her late husband's brother's orphaned children, caring for them as her own. I remember Lilaram's constant anxiety about Duru. When he was approached for her hand by Narayan's illustrious father, it was a great joy, but also a great worry as he had no money to buy her jewellery for her wedding.

It so happened that I was in their house when Lokumal and his wife arrived for the wedding. They came striding up the stairs, and Loku entered the room, hugged Lilaram, and said, 'Why are you worried? Here is the ring for Duru's marriage!' He took off his own wedding ring and handed it to him. Lilaram, overcome, burst into tears and clung to Loku, his body racked with sobs.

Those were the kind of family relationships in the Sindh of my childhood, and nothing has changed more in my world. Even the major changes in transportation, media and entertainment, and the even more dramatic changes in technology and communication, have had less impact on our lives than the changes in family structures and relationships!

Another thing I remember very clearly, even though it was so long ago, was the last few days spent at home before we left for Bombay. We had a large marble dining table which could seat ten people. Daddy gave that and our peengho to one of his Muslim friends. There was a picture frame of Krishna on the top beam and we unscrewed it before sending it to him. I remember how much my little sister Baby cried when she saw it being taken away. We packed all Daddy's books into big trunks and carried our clothes and some kitchen utensils in smaller ones.

Our first shock on the ship from Karachi to Bombay was the food. It was served on steel thalis, something we had never seen before, as in Sindh our plates and bowls were all made of bronze or kutta. And the puris were so tiny! We found that odd—in Sindh, we were used to proper large puris. We would soon have to get used to all this and more.

It was a three-day journey, but when the ship arrived in Bombay harbour, it was night, too late to dock. So we stayed on board another night. And then another. We did not know why we had been kept for an extra two days on the ship. Could it be that there was no tide? Or perhaps the authorities did not know what to do with yet another boatload of refugees and were trying to give themselves more time to prepare? These musings were accompanied by anxiety—were we going to be sent back? And if so, what would become of us? It was 14 November, 1947 when our ship docked in Bombay and we stepped out into the noisy, crowded city that was going to be our home.

My father was forty-two years old. In Hyderabad, he had already been acknowledged as one of the most prominent lawyers of Sindh. While our displacement could not have been easy for him, he was highly skilled and well-connected, and got a job immediately. A year later, he was appointed Magistrate of the Bombay Presidency, a prestigious and well-paying position. For us children, at first, everything was new and strange, and it was not hard to forget our homes and friends as we settled into new lives. Time passed, and we began getting news of our family members and friends who had also fled and settled in different places, and it was sad to know that some of them had had a much harder time than us.

About a month after we left, violent riots had broken out in Hyderabad. Dwarko's father was away in Jakarta and it was up to his mother to run with him, her aging parents-in-law, and her eighteen-year-old sister-in-law Rani, to the railway station, with nothing but the clothes on their back. They arrived in Ajmer after a harrowing journey during which Rani had somehow been tragically separated from them. They lived in abysmal conditions in a refugee camp—dirty, overcrowded, and with weevils in their food—for two months, until they were able to contact Dwarko's father and he made arrangements for them to join him in Jakarta. Two years later, Rani was spotted in Jaipur by one of our former neighbours in Sindh, sitting in ragged clothes with other beggars outside a temple. Dwarko's father arrived in Ajmer and took her home, but we later heard that Rani's eyes remained blank as she stared ahead of her, and she never spoke a single word for the rest of her life.

Pesu's family also left Hyderabad in December 1947. Ammi had packed some meagre belongings in a black tin trunk. The railway platform was crowded and a tall, hefty Pathan guard with an enormous moustache halted the frightened family to inspect what they were carrying out of the newly-formed Pakistan. He snatched open the trunk and stepped back when he saw, right on top, a framed picture of Saeen Sayed Malik. Kneeling in reverence, he offered a prayer, closed the trunk, and ordered his men to see Pesu's family safely into a compartment. It was, as Ammi always recounted it, a miracle wrought by Saeen Sayed Malik. The family settled in Bombay but the unfortunate Lilaram could not bear these forced changes and, in less than a year, he died.

As for Lila, we never saw her again. Her family had decided to stay on in Pakistan. Her new name was Ameena and I remember being told that she had been given in marriage to Imtiaz, whose father was a zamindar.

My brother Kanna, an extraordinarily brilliant and sensitive person, never really adjusted to our unwarranted exile from our ancestral homeland. He completed his education and became a lawyer but he took to drinking and, sad to say, never led a stable life. All of us in my family, despite our relatively smooth transition, were affected by the trauma of Partition in some way or another. One of my symptoms is the uneasiness that shrouds me many mornings when I wake up early and hear the aazaan ring out. It is a complicated, uncomfortable feeling that takes me back to when I was young and could see that my parents were scared and uncertain about what the future held. It takes time for my rational nature, my education, and the strong feeling of respect for all forms of worship native to us Sindhis, to slowly rise to the surface and comfort me. One day, as I gently eased myself towards a warmer and more positive feeling for the aazaan, I suddenly remembered my mother's tears when pallo was cooked, and I understood that it was her way of expressing sorrow for the lost home she knew she would never see again, for our land and its people, its sights and sounds.

For most of my adult life, I have lived in South India in very different circumstances from my childhood and my youth. I never again saw the kind of grand river that we took so much for granted when we were children. Sindh, unlike the rest of India, does not receive monsoon rains. If not for the Indus, which irrigates large parts of Sindh, it would be a desert. However, the Indus is known to change its course without warning. One year your home could be two miles from the river, the next the river might be running past your door; then, years would come in which your whole village would be washed away and you would have to move and start all over again. Perhaps this is what has made us Sindhis a people who are adaptable, resourceful, and cooperative; it is why we revere nature and respect human limitations.

So now you know quite a lot about my family, my childhood — and even my community! One thing that I have not yet told you is my name, as I was saving that for the end. When I was born, my parents named me Sati and that is what I was called all through my childhood in Sindh and ten subsequent years in Bombay. It was during my interview for the post of junior lecturer at the English Department of a college in Pune one morning in 1958 when the head of the department looked at her colleagues on the panel and asked with a supercilious sneer, '"Sati"! What kind of name is that?' And that is how I came to be known as Sita, the name by which I will be called till the day I die.

We Sindhi Hindus lost all our material possessions when we left Sindh. We worked hard and became prosperous again, but in this time-taking and energy-consuming process, we hardly even realized how much more we had lost: not just our ancestral roots and our culture, but even our language, because our parents, like insecure migrants the world over, preferred to equip us with the skills of local languages which would give us an advantage in our future lives. Most of us don't even know about the wealth of Sindhi poetry and philosophy that we should have rightfully inherited. And many, like me, even lost our names.

Saaz Aggarwal is a writer and artist based in Pune, India. Her body of writing includes biographies, translations, critical reviews and humour columns. Her books are in university libraries around the world, and much of her research contribution in the field of Sindh studies is easily accessible online.

The Lost Sky

Nina Sabnani

This is the story of how I came to have two homes. I was born in 1933, in British India, to Sugnichand and Devi Bagwani in Old Sukkur, Sindh, now in Pakistan. My father, Sugo Dada, as he was called, was the youngest of three brothers. They all lived in the same neighbourhood. That is how it was in those days. Sugo Dada and his wife Devi lived next door to Sugo's brother Mohini Dada, or the father of Mohini and his wife, Kala. Their eldest brother Lachmandas lived with his wife Sadori across the street. There was more than just the street that divided these households. The houses of Sugo Dada and Mohini Dada functioned like one big joint family, partly because Sugo was away a lot. He lived in Bawalpur, where he owned a petrol pump and a textiles colour agency. Devi was mostly by herself and so, she relied heavily on Kala for everyday domestic solutions. Devi and Kala shared errands and rooms, and courtyards where the women and children spent most of their day. Lachmandas's house was set apart, and the family somewhat aloof.

Lachmandas and Sadori did not have any children. Ever since I was born, they wanted to adopt me. This was not unusual for the time. My parents, on the other hand, were not too keen as I was their firstborn. After three daughters, however, my mother Devi could not refuse their earnest pleas. When I was six, I was taken from my home to the house across the street. I would now be living with my uncle and aunt and would soon learn to call them Baba and Suthi Amma or, the good mother. Baba was in the business of selling German Pfaff sewing machines in new Sukkur. It was the most popular brand in those days and most people sewed their own clothes at home. Baba was well-known for repairing machines as well. Back then, nobody threw anything away.

Sukkur was a neat town on the west bank of river Indus, known to us as the Sindhu nadi. It was famous for its barrage and Lansdowne Bridge. Since I moved to my new home, I would go every Sunday with Baba and Suthi Amma to Saadh Belo, which was an island in the middle of the river and boasted many temples. We would take a *beri* or boat to this place, climb the marbled steps to all the temples and eat the *langar*, a community meal. Once, I watched Sant Kanwarram sing and dance the *bhagat*, a kind of storytelling with dance and music. He wore a frockcoat with *churidaars* and had bells on his feet.

Our houses in old Sukkur had common walls between them, on the side and back, so that each house was only open on one side, at the entrance with a courtyard. The entrance door was always open but there was a wooden screen facing the entrance, so that no passerby could look inside. The entrance door was only locked at night. The terraces of each house were connected and were places where women and children could meet freely.

Hussaina was my best friend. She had the kindest face and a very warm smile. Our homes were connected back to back. Our terraces met, and this is where we would chat with each other, unobserved by the elders. Now, Suthi Amma was a little large and did not have the energy to climb the three floors up to the terrace, and so it was left to me to nimbly climb up to the terrace to put out the washing, put the freshly rolled *pappads* to dry in the sun or to air the *razais* on the *khat*, a cot made from ropes. I loved doing things around the house. Doing the chores offered the perfect excuse for me to run up to the terrace whenever I wanted to meet Hussaina to gossip, or exchange food, or learn crocheting. Theirs was a conservative family and Hussaina was not allowed to step out of her house without an escort. Hussaina's house also had a huge courtyard with date palm trees, where I would often go and play with Hussaina and her older sisters. We played *Wanjh Vati* or hopscotch and *Panjkila*, a game of five stones. These stones were either small smooth pebbles selected with care from the riverbank or the beautifully crafted painted ones in wood that Baba had got me from Haridwar. My most precious toy was the miniature kitchen utensils set that also came from Haridwar. I spent hours playing 'house' with my friends.

Each time Baba went away, he would bring me a new doll to add to my collection. I loved making clothes for my dolls, so one day, Baba brought home a sewing machine for me. Baba almost always indulged my every whim. When he needed to travel to Kolkata on business to see if he could acquire the dealership for Usha sewing machines, I insisted on going with him. He was reluctant because he thought it would be too cold. I packed my bag anyway but he left without me. I cried and cried and would not even speak to my Suthi Amma. Within hours, I saw that Baba had come back from the railway station! He had missed his train. Now he had no choice but to take me along with him the next day. It was the happiest day of my life, with just Baba and me.

It was like a big adventure. I was to see a world larger than our old little Sukkur. We went in our *buggie*, a horse carriage, to Rohri across the Sindhu nadi and from there, boarded a train for Lahore. From Lahore, we took a train to Amritsar, where we saw the Golden temple. From Amritsar, another train took us to Haridwar, where I saw the great Ganga. And from there, we travelled to Dehradun to see the magnificent Himalayas. Finally, we reached Kolkata. I had never seen such a place before. I had only read about such places in my school textbooks. This was so much better. Baba happily answered every question of mine and I could eat whatever I wanted without Suthi Amma's tight control. It was not like I did not love Suthi Amma, but it was so wonderful to be alone with my Baba.

We loved the trams in Kolkata. As soon as Baba's work was done, we spent all our evenings aimlessly going up and down in the trams. I was also happy to return home, as it's always nice to come back home. And I had so much to tell Suthi Amma, Hussaina and my school friend Kamla.

Kamla and I shared the same school bench in our classroom. We both loved dogs. Kamla had a Labrador she called Sheru. I so longed to have one too, but Suthi Amma wouldn't hear of it. So Kamla would bring him to meet me whenever she could.

I did not go across the street to Devi and Sugo Dada's house because Suthi Amma did not like it. But I went with Baba and Suthi Amma to their place for all our family get-togethers. Usually, these happened during festivals or when a new child was born. On such occasions, I would be curious about my 'cousins' and wanted to be friends with them, but Suthi Amma would discourage me from that, and on some pretext or another, she would bring me back home as soon as possible.

I was the happiest child, until one day, a day I will never forget for my whole life. I had just turned thirteen and was looking forward to moving to the English-medium school in our village. That fateful day, Baba called me and asked me to sit by his side. 'I have something to tell you,' he said in a soft gentle voice. 'You know I have loved you as a father,' he said. 'Yes, you have,' I replied. 'You are the best father in the whole world,' I told him. 'But I am not your father,' he said and looked away. 'Your parents are Sugo and Devi over at the other house and I am taking you to them tonight.' 'But you have always been my father!' I cried. 'Have I done something wrong Baba?' Baba said, 'It is for your own good, child.' He asked me to pack my things, but Suthi Amma said there was no need and that I could come back every day to bathe and dress. I wanted to ask them so many questions. I kept asking myself what I could have done to be punished like this. Suthi Amma would not look me in the eye.

That night I walked across the street with Baba. It was as if I was taking those few steps across the street with a total stranger. He stopped outside the door and asked me to call out to Devi. As usual, Sugo Dada was not at home, so Devi came to the window all covered in a veil and nodded her head. She did not say a word. Baba said to her, 'I am sorry, but I am returning your daughter to you. Partition may happen at any moment and I am not sure about my own safety. If anything were to happen to me, my wife will not be able to take care of Sheela the way she is used to. So please take care of her'. He almost cried as he said this and having said that, my precious Baba left without a second glance. I was confused. What was this Partition and why was he almost in tears, talking in riddles about his life and safety? I watched him leave till the moment when he shut the doors behind him of what had been my home, careful not to look at me.

Devi came out and nearly dragged me into the house. There were my 'cousins', staring at me shyly. Devi said, 'Sheela, these are your sisters Heeri and Savitri and this is your brother, Kanu'. I felt as if they were looking at me for the first time in our lives. I felt as if the whole world was staring at me and that I had nowhere to hide. Suddenly, I felt ill. I wanted to throw up. I went into the bathroom and cried my heart out. I was too sick to eat anything or speak to anyone. I just went to sleep on the bed given to me. I could feel many eyes watching as I got into the bed so I turned my face towards the wall and cried silently. Ever since, I have always cried silently.

The next morning, Suthi Amma sent for me to come and get dressed. I was thrilled. I bolted there in a second. I was sure that they wanted me back home. As it so happened, this was just an excuse for her to get me to run some errands. Was life back to normal? I did everything that she asked me to do happily. I ran up to meet Hussaina but Hussaina was not to be seen. I called out to her but a voice from the house said Hussaina was away. Baba too was away. Where was Baba? Where was Hussaina? They had all abandoned me. Was there no end to my misery? Devi called for me so I had to return to her house and help *her* with *her* chores. Suthi Amma looked so sad when I left. Now, I did not know which was my home. I was not homeless but neither house felt like home anymore.

Within a few days, Devi said I was not allowed to go to Suthi Amma's place. To make matters worse, one day, I found blood in my panties. Why was everything going wrong? Why was this happening to me? I could not think of one thing that I had done wrong to deserve this? Who could I tell about this awful thing now? I learnt about menstrual periods and the restrictions they came with from my aunt Kala. I could no longer attend school. Kala and Devi said that I must stay home and learn all the things a girl of thirteen ought to know. It was as if my whole life had fallen apart. I felt like nobody understood me and now, I could not leave the house unless accompanied by an elder either. I realized then how Hussaina might have felt at not being able to leave her house. Now, there was no way to meet her. When my school friend Kamla did not see me in class, she came around looking for me. Naturally, she was directed to the new house. She was surprised. It was as if almost overnight, I had become somebody else, almost unrecognizable. She promised to come by often but the look that Devi gave her told me that this would never happen.

Then a week later, Sugo Dada arrived and said we must start packing. It brought back memories of my travels with Baba. How I missed him and wondered if he ever thought of me. Are we going to Rohri to get the train? Devi muttered something about Partition and leaving our town forever. But why? No one would tell me. I did not have much to pack; all my things were at Suthi Amma's, where I was now forbidden to go. The street that divided the two homes was just a few feet wide, but now it seemed to have become a border between two countries.

Since Sugo Dada returned home, he had been listening to the radio quite a bit, and there was a lot of whispering among the elders. I could not quite follow what they were listening to and why they were whispering, but it must have been something very serious. Everyone was walking around looking anxious and worried.

And then one day, we just left in the middle of the night, packed in two cars and allowed to speak only in hushed whispers. It was the saddest day. I looked longingly at our houses and our street and the familiar paths I had walked on. Baba's house was in darkness, but I was sure someone was looking at us from the corner window. How could we leave just like that? Why did we have to leave at all?

Devi said we were taking a plane from another city. The thought of the plane took my mind off the questions that were hammering in my brain. We arrived at the Jacobabad airport within a few hours. I had never seen a plane before in my life. It was just for our two families, so there were no other people around. It was almost dawn when we took off. As the plane left the ground, my stomach lurched and I felt queasy. Just then, I saw the sun come up, all red and pink and orange, a fiery sight to remember forever. Everything grew distant and small, until all that remained of my homeland was the clouds. This feeling of being in the clouds has stayed with me since then and has consoled me whenever I have felt sad.

We arrived at Ahmedabad airport and then took a train to Udaipur. All this went by in a blur. In Udaipur, we lived in a house by the Pichola Lake where people spoke to us very harshly at first, and in a language different from the one we were familiar with. They called us '*sharnarthis*' or refugees. I wanted to go back home, and asked Devi, why were we staying in a house in Udaipur? It was then that Devi said that we were never going back. Never, ever? Then who would take care of our house? How could this be? Was Baba still there? Would I never see him again? Devi did not pay any attention to my questions.

One day, someone knocked on our door and it was Baba. My joy knew no bounds! I wanted to rush into his arms but something stopped me. He too seemed a bit shy. Tears welled up in our eyes as he tenderly stroked my head. He asked how I had been and I could see he looked very tired. The family gathered around him as he told us how he had come from Sukkur and his attempts to build a new business in the new land. He had come with loads of gifts and I shared them all with my 'cousins', whom I now knew as my brother and sisters. I wondered if Baba was going to take me back, but he did not say anything and nor did anyone else. He left, promising to come visit again.

We had hardly been in Udaipur for three months when it was time to move again, this time to Jodhpur. There, people were more friendly and hospitable. Even so, Sugo Dada could not find any work. Six months later, Sugo Dada and Mohini Dada moved us all to Jaipur. I had lost all sense of home completely. That is when I stopped giving a voice to the questions in my head. Instead, I started talking to myself. It was very comforting doing that. I found ways to explain to myself things that I did not understand. I found reasons to console myself about things that were difficult to bear.

In Jaipur, we lived in a place called Bani Park. Unlike our house in Sukkur, this house had its courtyard at the back. It was in a large plot surrounded by several flowering plants like mogra or jasmine which I loved. Once, I picked some to make myself a *gajra* for my hair but our landlord scowled, so I stopped. I wondered if Baba would visit me here too but no, he did not. One morning, a letter arrived for me! It was from him. He wrote how he still adored me as a daughter and that I could always write to him and tell him about my life and ask for anything I wanted. Writing to him helped me a lot. I wrote him all about the places we had moved in and out of and the kind of people we met and how they had treated us. Baba had started a business of selling firecrackers. Knowing how much I enjoyed fireworks, he sent me a Raavan stuffed with firecrackers. I stitched up the loose parts of the cloth Raavan and lit him on Dussera. Sparks of various colours lit up the sky as the different firecrackers exploded. I was so happy I had Baba in my life again.

Once, I wrote him that it made me miserable that I did not speak the language of the people in Jaipur and that I wanted to learn Hindi. I had not been sent to school since I had started living with Devi and Sugo Dada, but I was determined to learn on my own. Baba immediately sent me three dictionaries that would help me learn the new language so that I would feel more at home in this adopted city. The dictionaries became my best friends and between them and the radio, I taught myself many new things. The radio was not in our part of the house, so I had to do many errands for my aunt to be able to sneak out and listen to it.

In the process of learning to take care of my younger siblings and sharing chores with Devi and Kala, I learned many things. I learnt to sew clothes for my siblings and myself. Even though my aunt Kala taught me many things like cooking and knitting, she was reluctant to teach me how to cut patterns for the clothes.

I had to learn how to cut cloth on my own and I had found an ingenious way of doing just that. I would take apart old clothes with a needle and cut the cloth using the old ones as a template. One day, Sugo Dada saw me taking apart a garment and felt so sorry for me that he got a tailor to cut the patterns so I did not have to labour so hard. But I would still cut the patterns myself for some special things. I realized the cloth needed to be ironed flat to be able to cut properly. In one of my letters to Baba, I wrote about not having an iron. On my fifteenth birthday, a coal iron was delivered to the house for me. Soon, Sugo Dada got me my own radio so I did not have to fight with the others to listen to my favourite programmes on the BBC Hindi service and Voice of America. Even though they were not always present, in the end, I had two fathers who looked out for me. I made new friends but I think I was my own best friend. Even though I did not go to school, I managed to teach myself by learning from the radio and observing my aunt Kala and Devi as they went about their daily chores. They had their own struggles and we all did our best to get along as well as a big joint family possibly could.

I often thought about my home far away and wondered about Hussaina and Kamla. I thought about my home with the terrace where I would play for hours with Hussaina, sharing food and books. I don't have anything from the home I left behind except these memories. And in my memories, I will always have my two homes, just like I have both my Baba and Sugo Dada.

Nina Sabnani is an artist and storyteller who uses film, illustration and writing to tell her stories. Her research interests include exploring the dynamics between words and images in storytelling. She has received several awards including the National Award in 2016 for her animated film Hum Chitra Banate Hain and the lifetime achievement award for Illustration at the Tata Lit Live Festival at Mumbai in 2018.

Mind your Language

Dushyant

It was a warm summer morning in the year 2040. It was a unique case, and possibly the first of its kind in the court. The courtroom of the senior Judge Sahab was jam-packed. At exactly 11 am, the Judge Sahab came out of his chamber and sat down on the assigned seat. His assistant in the court read out the case details and informed him about the two contesting parties.

Spitting the *paan* into the spittoon, the Judge Sahab signalled for court proceedings to commence.

The public prosecutor Sikandar Sahil started,

'My Lord! It's a simple case. As His Highness is aware, as per the ruling government's new law formed by the approval of the bill in the parliament, the languages in the country today have a clear leaning and association towards specific religions. This leaves very few languages that are religion-neutral, English being one of those.'

'His Highness knows well that the young ones who chose to pursue literature and linguistics for languages other than the ones associated with their religion now face the storm as their degrees stand null and void. Even the courts have been directed that a Hindu must speak Hindi and a Muslim must stick to Urdu. However, if they wish, they both could well choose English for communication. The courts have been awarded some grace period within which the lawyers will have to decide their affinities.

Well, that's not all, they even have to get it registered as the language for their future practice.'

The judge interrupted, 'Cut it short! What's the main agenda here?'

The lawyer said, 'That's exactly what I am coming to. Sir, now, as per the law, Hindi is solely reserved for Hindus, Sanskrit for Brahmins, Urdu for Muslims and Punjabi for Sikhs. The man being interrogated, called Pankaj Singh, is a science teacher. He is a Hindu only by birth as his acquired language is Urdu and he takes immense pride in this; even his social media expressions are in Urdu. This has become objectionable to the intellectuals from either side. And I wish to bring this objection to light, my lord. The case has solid ground. If not addressed and resolved tactfully, the matter can lead to huge social unrest in the country.'

'My lord, I would also like to submit the write-ups, prints of social media posts as well as a copy of *Andhere Dinon me Chirag* by Pankaj Singh as proof to validate my charges.'

The judge said, 'What does the defending lawyer, Mr Kabir Mukul, have to say to this?'

'Dear Sir, the case isn't as simple and as clear as is being made out to be! I strongly condemn the charges as the languages of this country have never been associated with a specific religion. Languages have always belonged to regions and groups. My client is innocent!'

'But how can a Hindu claim Urdu as his language, especially with the new law in practice?'

'My lord, may I know the language the court is following?' asked Kabir Mukul.

Irked by his question, the judge replied, 'The same that's being used right now! Is there some kind of a joke going on?'

'Absolutely, sir! If I were to say the same about the case, it will be an insult to the honourable court.'

The judge instructed, 'Let Pankaj Singh record his statement.'

'My client wants to swear on his grandfather's diary!' The judge nodded in affirmation to the request made by defending lawyer Kabir Mukul, whose French-cut beard and rimless spectacles were adding to his charm.

'My name is Pankaj Singh, s/o Surendra Singh, Mukam-Post- Thana Gopiwala. I am a teacher by profession. I have not committed any crime. I strongly believe that my preferred language is definitely not from the other religion. I consider this as my own. This is how my parents, my senior generations spoke. In fact, I distinctly remember, my grandfather's letter written to my father had a distinct Urdu flavour, despite being scripted in Devnagari. Yes, the very starting words were "*mere lakht-e-jigar.*"'

Kabir said, 'The diary on which my client swore is written in Urdu, my lord.'

Sikandar Sahil interrupted, 'My lord, all these things have no bearing on the case. These attempts are being made to waste our precious time. In fact, all these things clearly make Pankaj guilty. The case is so clear and convincing that, without any delay, the court can declare him guilty today itself.'

The judge said, 'Court proceedings are not to be taken lightly. It is not possible. The court requests PP to present his witness and arguments.'

'Yes sir,' PP alias Sikandar Sahil nodded in affirmation.

The witness was called out—a Pandit, Tansukh Chaturvedi alias Tarun Sharma.

Dressed in jeans with a tika on his forehead, the young Pandit came to the witness box. The *Ramcharitmanas* was brought and he did the customary swearing.

'I am Tansukh Chaturvedi.'

'You seem to be a smart guy, but why would you have two names?'

'You know, I was named Tansukh by my grandfather and my father didn't like this traditional name so he named me Tarun.

But my original name did help me in getting a job, as people took me more seriously with that name.'

'That's fine! Your professional secrets need no more light. But we need to understand your reservations against Pankaj Singh.'

'Sir, you need to understand, if everyone started behaving like Pankaj, the situation will become catastrophic.'

'May I say something, sir?' intervened Kabir Mukul.

'Sure, go ahead! Do you have any questions for Pandit Ji?'

'Thank you, sir! Pandit Ji, just tell me if the country was suffering before this law was enforced?'

'Sir, a wise and sensible ruler would always work proactively and make decisions that are favourable for his people.'

'Don't forget that the country has democracy and the courtroom you are standing in right now is being governed by the rules of democracy. To compare it with a monarchy will be wrong.'

'I beg your pardon, sir! I actually meant the government. So, I humbly request that when the government has passed a law in purview of social harmony, to guide and lead the youth of the nation towards religion and culture and to maintain the high moral grounds, then every citizen must abide by the law. And any citizen going against it should be reprimanded.

'In my opinion, Pankaj Singh has committed a grave crime and he should be held guilty without any delay.'

'Thank you, you may take your seat Pandit Ji!' said the judge while noting down the points, and asked the defending lawyer to contest the charges.

Kabir Mukul, in his typical style, started, 'My first witness is the renowned linguist and Urdu scholar, Professor Saxena. It's worth mentioning that his father and his grandfather served as the *Diwan* to the Hindu monarch. Professor would like to swear on a copy of the *Deewan-e-Ghalib*.'

Average height, a grey moustache, and a pair of sparkling bright eyes peeping through a broad frame. His maroon *kurta*, *choodidar payjama* and smartly polished leather sandals spoke volumes about his impressive personality.

Sikandar Sahil objected—'I object, my lord! How can one swear on a copy of the *Diwan-e-Ghalib*?'

The judge replied, 'Objection overruled! Please don't forget that this is quite valid unless there is a law stating otherwise. In fact, it's as valid as a lover swearing on his love letters for his beloved.'

The courtroom was filled with laughter.

'Order, Order, Order. Carry on Professor, what do you have to say?'

So, as per the practice, the Professor pledged to abide by the truth and he continued.

'Trust me, I am a fan of yours. The world of Urdu laureates and scholars holds you in very high regard, sir.'

'Oh, but what have I done to earn this?' asked the judge.

Sikandar Sahil interrupted, 'Excuse me, my lord! All this is just aiming to while away the crucial time of the court.'

He wasn't sparing a chance to be critical of Kabir Mukul.

'I am convinced that my dear friend is heavily inspired by Mumbai filmi plots where, for the lack of a solid repartee, the counsel often resorts to similar lame excuses. The truth is that if there is a solid case then arguments and discussions are bound to happen.'

The glance from the judge was enough to embarrass Sikandar. Kabir was, of course, elated.

Professor continued, 'You are well known for quoting Urdu shayars in your remarkable judgements. All newspapers carry these as headlines. Your love and passion for Urdu need no validation, sir.'

The judge couldn't contain his smile. However, controlling his emotions, he carried on.

'I have been instructed by the high command about the sensitivity and the criticality of this case. The case has to be expedited. So please be crisp, precise and stay focused. Any unnecessary argument may delay this case indefinitely or go against it.'

While all this was going on, Judge Sahab noticed a pigeon that had placed itself on a stationary fan towards the end of the courtroom. Well, who knew if the pigeon had also got interested in the case? Pigeons are, as it is, believed to have an affinity to places of worship and intellect...

Kabir Mukul apologized to the judge and then addressed Mr Saxena, 'Sir, please be concise and brief as we don't have hours to discuss this.'

'*Huzoor*, I am a living testimony to the fact that the language I speak needs no religious validation. It holds at least two hundred years of historical validation.'

'Please be direct! You seem to be a sensible man,' the judge interrupted as he sipped some water.

'*Huzoor*, what did you just say?'

'Who do you think is the judge here? Now you have a counter-question for me?'

'*Huzoor*, what I am saying has a direct bearing on the case. Please answer my question.'

'Ok! All I said was, "*Paheliyon me baat na karein, seedhi karein, tameez wale lagte hain aap, phir bhi*"' (Please be direct! You seem to be a sensible man). The court has no time for such ambiguous and indirect discussions.'

'Just pay attention to what you just said, "*Paheliyon me baat na karein, seedhi karein, tameez wale lagte hain aap, phir bhi.*" Can you identify how many of the words in the sentence belong to Hindi and how many to Urdu?'

'Professor! You are now irritating me!'

'Yes, my lord! I am a bit irritating. Please excuse me for saying this, but you are a proud Hindu, so you will have to refrain from using Urdu words. Even the commonly spoken words. It's as simple as that.'

The judge began to make sense of all that was being said. He picked up his pen and then asked Professor Saxena,

'Do you have anything to say in favour of the accused?

'Absolutely! I beg your pardon again, but the court is applying this law to an individual whereas the case really doesn't belong to an individual.'

'What do you mean? Don't you think your wordplay is making the case unduly complicated?'

Reading the judge's reaction, Sikandar Sahil softened his stance, 'This is exactly what I meant. The gentleman is just wasting precious time. I request you to stop the proceedings right away.'

'No Sir! I understand the sanctity of this courtroom and I dare not disrespect the seat of the law. It's just that this case is distinct and a little unusual, so the arguments are bound to be a little different. And as we are aware the case has a linguistic bearing, I would therefore like to read out a few parts from the story of a writer. Please allow me.'

'You may proceed!'

'Thank you very much, sir. So, there is a story and I am quoting a line that is, "*Qismat ki chadar ka koee rafoogar nahin hai*" and then there is another one, "*Ameeri ki kabr par panapti huee gareebi badi zehreeli hoti hai.*"

Another excerpt from the same story is "*Isi ghodi ki badaulat unki tarakki rah gayi, lekin aakhiri dum tak vah afsaron ke ghaple me n aaye- har taraf se kaabil, mehnati, imandar, chalak, diler aur mustaid aadmi hote hue bhi vaha daroga ke daroga hi rah gaye- sirf ghode ki mohabbat se.*"'

I beg to know if there is anyone in this courtroom who can tell me the language in which this story is written. Can anyone tell me who the writer is? At least identify the language?'

'This is undoubtedly Urdu! The same that our accused Pankaj Singh has been using for his expression.' Sikandar was ecstatic while claiming this. Professor Saxena started smiling.

'Professor, no more wasting time please.'

'*Huzoor*, these excerpts are from the renowned author Shivpujan Sahay's story titled *Kahani Ka Plot*. I humbly request each one present here to filter out Urdu from these quotes and see what remains. I bet the entire meaning, the flavour, the plot will be lost.'

'Objection, my Lord! This is rather unreasonable of the defence lawyer to prove the guilty innocent. How can a piece of literature be presented as a witness?' shouted Sikandar Sahil.

'Thank you, Professor Saxena!'

On hearing this from the judge, Professor walked to his seat away from the witness box and sat down comfortably with his legs crossed.

'Now, you may call the Maulvi Sahab,' ordered the judge.

Maulvi Ahmad Ali Shah's name was called out and in no time, he was in the witness box. He swore on the Quran followed by *salaam*.

'So Maulvi Sahab, what's your view on Pankaj Singh? Do you consider him guilty?'

'Of course, without any doubt.'

'Why?'

'I agree with Panditji totally.'

'That's amazing. Really heartening to know that you and Panditji both agree on this matter. Wish this was so for all other matters too.'

'*Janab*, I am not joking. We may be from different religions but the adverse impact of him using the language of the other religion on ours is just the same.'

'Thank you, Maulvi Sahab!'

'Sikandar Sahil Sahab, if both the witnesses had to say the same thing, you also ended up wasting the time here. Just what you accused Kabir Mukul of.'

'What?'

'Wasting the time!'

'Order, order, order!'

'Maulvi Sahab, we have learnt that your son is pursuing his PhD in Sanskrit; is this true?'

Maulvi wasn't prepared for this and one could clearly sense his nervousness.

'Yes, yes this is true but the fact is that my family has disowned him for this very reason now. We are not even on talking terms. In fact, he is likely to lose all rights of inheritance to my property very soon.'

'Thank you, Maulvi Sahab. You may present a linguist from your side, Mr Sikandar Sahil.'

'I would like to call Prof. Dayakrishna Pandey.'

'Please proceed.'

Formally dressed in a grey coat, pants, an off-white shirt and a tie, this man in his sixties walked towards the witness box. Placing his palm on the holy book, the *Geeta*, he pledged to abide by the truth.

'Respected Judge Sahab, have you seen the film *Titanic*?'

'Is this some kind of a joke? First a story and now the film? What's going on?'

'I dare not, sir! But please tell me if you have seen the film. I am sure you must have heard about the Titanic ship for sure.'

'Yes, I have seen the film and also know about the ship.'

'I knew it! I was really confident of your sensibilities, sir.'

'I must say I am flattered, but I would rather have you directly come to the point and clarify your point in relation to Pankaj Singh's case.'

'Sir, all I want you to do is focus on the iceberg the ship had collided with. Who had anticipated such a huge iceberg underneath the water?'

By now, the judge had almost given up.

'I think I am losing it now.'

'Sir, in linguistics there is a theory called the Iceberg Theory that has a direct bearing on the case. It's an age-old theory. Just like the iceberg that had such huge depth underneath the surface, our languages have a really deep bearing on our culture and expression.'

Professor Saxena shouted from his chair, 'This is a total misinterpretation of the theory.'

'Please continue, Professor Pandey, your logic is interesting.' The judge impulsively said this and immediately controlled his tone by saying,

'I mean, please complete your thought.'

'So, a language is not and should not be treated as a tool in isolation. There is a certain behaviour, tradition as well as philosophy attached to it. This new law is just a way of reinforcing this fact. And, I also consider Pankaj Singh guilty as he is trying to attempt the impossible by merging the two extremes. This is not only impossible but illegal as well.'

The courtroom once again was abuzz with laughter.

'Order, order, order!'

'Objection, my lord,' said Kabir Mukul.

'Objection sustained.'

'*Huzoor*, Professor Pandey is speaking from a community's perspective. Pankaj Singh's expression as well his culture are the same. So this case has no connection with his theory.'

'Hmm. Next witness in the defence, please!'

'*Huzoor*, my next witness is Pankaj Singh's mother Sumitra Singh,' Kabir Mukul said.

She asked for *Kabirvani* to pledge for speaking the truth.

'The language of expression of my son is the same that all elders in my family have been speaking in for years. His grandparents, uncles, aunts.'

Sikandar Sahil interrupted, 'And now, this won't be possible any more.'

'But why?' the mother questioned.

'The language in which you are speaking has been granted to Muslims. You, being a Hindu, can't use it any longer.'

Puzzled, Sumitra Singh asked, 'So, are we expected to learn a new language at this age?'

'Yes, maybe that's the only way out. Either you change your religion or your language.'

'Sir, the country also has very stringent conversion laws. Changing one's religion isn't as easy anymore,' chuckled Kabir Mukul.

'Religion, one can't change. Language, one can't speak! What chaos has the country landed herself into?' said Sumitra Singh.

'Thank you, Sumitra Singh Ji,' said the judge.

And then he addressed Pankaj Singh:

'Don't you think that you are committing a crime?'

'No, not at all. The country has produced many Hindus who have taken well to Urdu and similarly innumerable Urdu *shayars* who are revered in the Hindi literary world.'

'Anyway, all that is a thing of the past now. What if the court now ordered you to write strictly in Hindi?'

'*Janab*, are you referring to the Hindi script? If that be the case, then it is fine.'

'No, I am referring to the spoken word. Meaning, the actual spoken usage of the language.'

'*Janab*, in that case, I may probably have to quit writing.

Sikandar Sahil was quick to intervene.

'*Huzoor*, the writer is not only headstrong, but he is also rude. He is constantly arguing with you. This shows sheer disrespect of the court on his part. You must reprimand him immediately.'

The judge started smiling. 'I think you have run out of arguments, Sikandar Sahab.'

'*Huzoor*, my argument is very simple. There is a new law introduced by the government and this gentleman has gone against it. He is guilty and deserves to be penalized and convicted. Simple! A fair judgement will set an example for the common public.

All the proofs submitted before the court are enough to pass a judgement and convict the accused.'

Baffled by this, the judge reacted, 'Please do not interfere in my work. Let me decide whether the accused is guilty or not.'

The deafening silence of the courtroom ended when suddenly, the fan at the back of the courtroom started up without giving the pigeon time to fly off. Within no time, the blood-soaked pigeon lay dead on the ground.

The judge asked the peon to take care of it, 'You just get the electrician to fix this at the earliest. Its erratic functioning is a cause of concern and the weak-hearted like me may suffer dearly.'

The courtroom was in splits.

'Order, order, order! So, Mukul Sahab, any other witness from you?'

'Yes, my lord! Just two more witnesses please.'

'Please proceed.'

Abdul Hasan, the next witness, was called.

A good looking, aged man was in the witness box, and he chose to swear on the book *Baba Farid Ki Kafiyan.*

'So, Mr Hasan, what do you do?'

'Apna transport ka business hai ji. Apne 4 truck chlde hain ji

(I am a transporter. I own 4 trucks)', he said in his heavy Punjabi accent.

'You speak Punjabi?'

'Punjabi taan meri das pushtan boldi rahi hai ji, batware to pailan assi odar seege. Lhande Punjab! Punjabi sadi ma boli hai ji.'

(Yes, Punjabi is what my ancestors spoke. Before Partition, we were in Punjab. Punjabi is our mother tongue, sir.)

'But you are a practising Muslim, right?'

'Haan ji, panj waqat da namazi. Haan, abbu pichle saal hajj vee jaake aaye ne! Tussi hairan ho? Tuhanu nahi pata Kazi Nazrul Islam Bangladesh de vadde shayar si, te onna di zubaan taan

Bangla si. Te hor suno ji, vathere sardar hai ji, jehde urdu vich likhd ne, arbi , farsi jaande ne, hun o vi nahi bol, padh, likh sakan ge ji?'

(Yes, sir. Proudly a 5-times-a-day *Namazi*. My father did the Haj just last year. Don't be surprised! Don't you know that the first language of Kazi Nazrul Islam, the famous Bangladeshi poet, was Bangla? And what about the many Sikhs I know who know Urdu, Arabic and Persian. What about them? They won't be spared either?)

'Well, that's what the new law says. Thank you, Hasan Sahab,' said the judge.

Hasan left the witness box and moved towards his seat.

The next call was for Arindam Bhattacharya. And he chose to swear in the name of *Shri Shri Ram Krishna Kathamrat*.

'Pronam sir. Mera naam Arindam Bhattacharya hai. Hindi amko jada nahi aata hai. Am bongali manush. Khoob bhodro manush. Ye bokil Sahab *bola amko ki am idhar aake aapse pooch sakta ki am hindu hai to amko Hindi hi bolna padega. Ee shob cholbe na dada. Aami jani na.'*

(Hello sir! My name is Arindam Bhattacharya. I am not very fluent in Hindi. I am an ordinary Bengali man. The lawyer told me to check with you that being a Hindu now, I can speak only in Hindi. But how will I manage, I really do not know much Hindi.)

Sikandar interrupted, 'How dare you speak Bangla, being a Hindu? That too in the courtroom. You can actually be put behind bars!'

Amaara saat peedhi se jyada Bangla ee bolta hai. Am hindu hai par aamaara bhasha to Bangla.

(We have been speaking Bangla for almost seven generations now. We are Hindus but our language is Bangla).

Kabir Mukul commented, 'My lord, I request you to record Arindam Bhattacharya's testimony and his statement.'

The judge started writing on the paper and said, 'The court is adjourned till tomorrow. The verdict shall be out tomorrow.' And with this, he left for his chamber.

The next day, the court premises was bustling with crowds. The old electrician was busy repairing the fan. He started cleaning the bloodstain from the blade of the fan. One could make out from the lens on his glasses that he had poor vision. People were passing him by to enter the courtroom.

Judge Sahab came out of his chamber and sat down on his assigned seat. After aiming the *paan* towards the spittoon, he joined his hands, looked at the faded picture behind him, and started speaking amidst the chaos.

'Order, order, order! So, finally, the day of judgement for this unique case has arrived. I have patiently listened to both parties. It was interesting to listen to the defending party for all the right reasons. Actually, this case in itself is extremely interesting and historic. And the line between the right and wrong judgement here is going to be very thin. I am not sure for how many more days I am going to grace this seat. Who knows if this turns out to be my last judgement!

'So, I order the parliament to pay a penalty of One Rupee and I strongly suggest that such senseless laws that just waste the precious time of the court shouldn't ever be made.'

The next day, the headline in the newspaper read,

'A pigeon loses life to a speeding fan in the courtroom.'

Apparently, the delay in the news was caused as the reporter of the legal cell was on his weekly day off. The news piece was full of emotion. At the end of this piece, in the last column, was a brief saying that the judge had been expelled and arrested for dishonouring the government's law.

And there was no mention of the development that Pankaj Singh was brutally beaten up by the mob outside the court and was admitted to Mahatma Gandhi Hospital.

Translated from the Hindi by Harsh Pant

Dushyant writes lyrics and scripts for Hindi cinema. His first collection of short stories *July ki Ek Raat* was published by Penguin in 2013. His first novel *Via Gurgaon* was published by Juggernaut in 2016. Rajkamal Prakashan published his doctoral thesis in History in 2012.

New Directions

Uma Krishnaswami

My grandmother stirs early, even for her. She shuffles noisily out to milk the buffaloes. By the time I'm half-awake and stumbling to my feet, the milk is already poured into the district dairy collection jugs, which we must fill at the price they set if we are to stay in business. The meagre rest, we save for our tea and buttermilk.

Nanima and me, bound to each other ever since my parents died in the last of the Indo-Pak wars, fifteen years ago. I survived only because Nanima packed me up—little me, six months old—and took off before the attacks began.

Which side unleashed the single death-cloud? Each accused the other. It was limited, they agreed. A limited nuclear exchange? Tell that to the people it vaporized.

For five years, we hid in ancient caves, along with Salima's family and several dozen others, foraging for food and water. By the time we returned, whole towns had been flattened, but the stench of death had cleared. Grass was growing back. The buffalo herd had shrunk, but the old queen was still alive, although missing an eye. How did they escape the blasts? No one knew.

Nanima says I must leave here and find a better life. Only, how can I leave her alone in this place, where war has shattered the climate and the land?

Salima says now, with the border truce, the cities are rebuilding. We should go. Purvigram? Shamalshahr? Take your pick.

In those places, she says, no one has to get up to milk buffaloes at dawn. People live in the same house the whole year round, just imagine! Never mind if it's rainy or hot or growing season. No packing everything and taking the herd to find new grazing grounds, two-three months at a time. We could go to college. Learn things. Not the useless things they teach in school, like reciting the Indo-Pak wars and the causes of climate decline.

Skills. That's what we need, she says. Think about it.

I'm thinking about it as Nanima and I haul the milk jugs to the collection point, where a dairy employee receives them. The milk lorry's not here yet. The dairyvala counts our jugs, pays us in the usual multicoloured stack of notes, and waves us away as if we smell bad.

Salima says water comes to city houses all by itself, no collection tanks, no filtration ponds, no checking for contaminants. We'll get jobs. We'll be as good as anyone.

Nanima drags her feet. 'Are you all right?' I ask her.

She mutters, 'Couldn't sleep last night. My treacherous mind, Payal. It won't stay still.'

My own mind is never still. I have to keep it roaming all the time, just to live. In the salty desert, half-flooded from the last two sea-risings, I'm always watching for something. Bandits. Hyenas. Circling vultures that spiral down to earth to pick the wild cow carcasses clean. If the vultures are busy, I don't have to worry about the cheetahs who abandoned those carcasses.

'Go, go,' Nanima says. 'Go to school.'

She believes school is my ticket to a better life. What would she think of today's visiting boss from the Public Safety Department? He tells us how hard the government is working to mitigate the effects of WWDs (Weapons of Widespread Destruction). 'We're planning a new disposal site. Vital work...national security...create jobs...young people must be gainfully employed.'

'What jobs?' Salima whispers.

'Digging holes,' I whisper back, 'to bury poisons.'

A teacher warns us we are talking too much.

Gujarati-Hindi-Maths-History. When the school day is done, we plod home in discontent. 'I'm telling you,' Salima says, 'One day, soon, we'll be gone from here...'

I stare into the end of school in a few more weeks, our future looming ahead. We've never known a time when we didn't know each other. Since our return, we've grazed cattle and buffaloes in the grasslands and swamps and abandoned fields for a hundred kilometres around. Two families with different gods and different ways, helping each other in this land that war and weapons have spoiled for everyone.

What will happen to us?

At the end of my path, there's Nanima in the doorway of the dilapidated roundhouse, our home for four months every year. She scans the sky, mostly brilliant blue with a few scraps of cloud.

'Lightning?' I ask. Will ocean winds blow rain our way?

She shakes her head. 'Not yet, but listen.' She leans her tired back on the carved wooden doorway, rubbed smooth by generations of hands.

At first, I can't hear anything. Then noisy wings flap overhead. Clawed feet scuttle over the roof. Beaked heads appear on the rim; bright eyes peer down at us. 'The crows are nesting,' says Nanima.

I shake my head. The crows are thieves. They steal our grain. When Nanima hangs her odhni out to dry, they peck the beads from it and carry them to their nests for decoration. My grandmother says nesting crows foretell the rain. I don't think that's been true for the last century.

If it rains now, our little crop of millet and vegetables will survive. We'll need the grain for the dry season, when the land will cake and crack and we herders must leave again.

I am tired of leaving and returning, year after year. I am tired of depending on rains that spit down upon us whenever they wish, their wishes drifting in the wind.

Salima has planted a vision in my eyes of water arriving in pipes, gushing out, sparkling, spraying silver. As much as we need, any time, free of poisons. It's a dream.

'I heard they've got the dams working again,' I venture. 'In Khari and Nirona. Think we'll get that water here one day?'

Nanima looks at me sideways, just like the crows. 'Don't be a fool,' she says. 'Why do we need their water, or their power, or their anything?'

What's wrong with enough water and power? Enough that I don't have to keep checking the water level in the tank, or the connections that anchor the sun-sheets on our roof. What is wrong with wanting enough and maybe a little more?

Nanima says, 'When you leave here. you'll understand.'

She always pushing this future for me—somewhere else. How can I leave without her? She says if I take her to a city, pin her down to a single place, the breath will go out of her.

This isn't an argument I can win. 'I'll take the animals out,' I say.

'Come straight back,' she cautions. I make a face at her, inviting a glare.

By the time I open the compound gate, Rani, the one-eyed queen buffalo, is stamping her foot. She rumbles a scolding: *Late, late,* she's telling me. *You're late.* She pushes past, showing me who's in charge. Once she's out, the rest fall in line and follow her.

My grandmother can take a sip of milk and tell which of the animals it came from. She says some of them give sweeter milk than others. I think Rani's always tastes like onions. When I tell Nanima that, she laughs and says, affectionately, 'She's an old demon, that one.' Sometimes I wonder, how poisoned is this milk? It's not a question to ask out loud. Everything is poisoned. The air, the water.

Between rows of houses, many empty, a few children play in the dust, whooping and laughing, drawing circles with sticks. Not many families remain. Who can stay for drought one year and floods the next and half the land unfit to live upon?

Buffalo bodies trudge around me, their sour smells rising in the warm air. They are unstoppable, heading for fodder. A calf's wet nose nuzzles me in passing. I pat a tough hide. I move with them and don't break free until we have crossed the dry riverbed to the grassland.

Now, the herd doesn't need me. They move on, single-minded, bent on finding small patches of green to tear up and chew, swallow, regurgitate, and chew all over again. It's a day-long job. After they're done, Rani, their queen, will lead them home at sunset, avoiding the toxic spots where nothing grows.

We've lived this way for centuries, Nanima says, us and the buffaloes, with a queen in every herd: one stubborn female who knows her way and won't do as she is told.

The grasses are pale in the sunlight, tiny diamonds of salt glistening on their blades. The buffaloes in this land are the only ones who can eat this salty grass and live.

A spiny lizard scurries out of my way, and that is when I notice something I've never seen before. Someone has planted small tufts of grass in this wild place. Someone has covered them with nets to protect them from grazing cattle. Someone has sprinkled water on these baby grasses.

I should go back but I too, don't do as I am told.

Instead, I follow the seedlings, from one clump to the next, until I'm sweating. My lips are salty, my eyes and nostrils itchy and dry. Then I spot someone squatting down, putting something small and green in the ground, among the grasses, in a clearing of thorny gando bawal trees.

'Alibhai Kaka? What are you doing here?' It's Salima's father.

He springs up in alarm, then relaxes when he sees it's only me.

'What's all this?' A wooden box beside him is packed with bunches of grass seedlings, each growing out of a little earth plug. From a tall milk jug, he sprinkles water on the new plantings.

'Grass,' he says. 'Been putting it in since we came back. We collect the seeds and germinate them at home, then plant again.' He tells me about the grassland, how it should dry out every year, then swell with water when the rains come, growing food enough for cattle and birds. 'That's how it's supposed to be.'

For more than a century, the government thought the land was good for nothing. 'When I was a boy, they sent helicopters up to scatter thorn tree seeds. From South America, can you believe? Supposed to improve the land.'

How tender those seedlings are, how green. He lifts his arms as if he wants to hold them all, grass and land and sky. 'They saw only wasteland. But once, there were fifty different kinds of grass. Sixteen species of lizards. A hundred kinds of birds.'

I know all this. I also know that fifty years after the seed-scattering, the Environment Ministry decided the gando bawal were bad after all and spread poison to kill them. It didn't work. The mad trees are still everywhere, sticking us with their thorns, draining the water, drying out the grass that keeps Rani and the herd alive. And then the war. What can survive all that?

'What use is it?' I ask. 'One seedling, or five, or fifty?'

'See how it holds fast to the ground?' He tugs a clump. 'Those roots join the roots of other plants. See? It won't let me pull it out!'

He says he's not the only guerilla gardener. 'We have quite a few. They catch us, fine us, threaten us with jail. All for planting seeds.'

'You really think this is going to—'

'Heal the land?' he says. 'It's life holding onto life. If we help them, they'll grow. They'll help each other grow.'

He gives me a searching look. 'How much do you know? About your parents? You were just a baby.'

'They went to college,' I say. 'They came back to help Nanima. They were—my parents.' I see it in his face. I know nothing.

'Payal,' he says, 'ask your Nanima. It's time she told you.'

'She's part of—this?' I think of Nanima going out on long walks, leaving me to handle meals. Nanima protecting trays of green sprouts from the sun. I'd thought they were vegetables she was taking care of for the neighbours. I see patterns I never saw before.

He nods. 'We have to be careful. We don't own this land, you see, so we are not allowed.'

Of course we don't own it. No one does. The grassland is just—grassland. For everyone. Isn't it?

'These days, mostly, they've stopped bothering us. They have bigger plans.' He digs a new hole with his pointed khodali. 'See here. If—when—the rains come, the seedlings will survive and the grassland will grow...' He gestures around him. 'A lot of this is from two years ago. If we just had time...'

What does it take to tend a grassland the way you'd tend potatoes and onions? Who does it take? '*Nanima* comes out here?'

'She used to. Not as much now.' A shadow crosses his face. 'What can I say? Soon it will all be stories. This may be the last planting.'

'Why?' I cry.

'They're going to build a cleanup site here,' he says.

'Cleanup?'

Vital work. It can create jobs. Mitigation. Jobs. *What jobs?* we'd joked, Salima and I.

He presses earth around the sweet green handful. He waters it, a wet earth scent rising from the ground. 'The land can live again but only if we let it.'

By the time I get back, my mind is whirling like a dozen helicopters.

'What took you so long?' Nanima says.

I tell her about the secret grass seedlings. 'Alibhai Kaka said...I should ask you. About Ma and Papa.'

'Your Ma and Papa?' she mumbles. Of course, who else? Are they stones in her mouth, my parents, that she can't bear to talk about them?

'Nanima!' I cry. 'I'm old enough to know. What were they doing? What did he mean, it's time you tell me? Tell me what?' I am angry now. I have to know.

Her face crumples. 'They didn't die in the war,' she says.

'But you told me—'

'I know. I couldn't...you were so little.'

'So tell me now,' I beg.

'Payal, potri.' She reaches up to take a pot down from the corner niche, where it sits in front of a mirror-decorated cloth embroidered with a Ganesh image.

The matti pot is Nanima's great-grandmother's. That puts it—what?—six generations before me, all the way back to old India in the time of the Angrez. 'He's right,' she says. 'It's time to tell you now.'

For years, I have seen Nanima take that pot down, clean it up, and put it back. When we go away for the dry season, she packs it carefully and takes it along. It's the first thing she unpacks on every return.

She dusts it now as if she's shining up her memory. Then she tips the pot so I can look inside. It's full of seeds.

'I plant them for her,' she says. 'Your mother loved the grasslands. The birds, the little wildflowers that bloomed after the rains, even the snakes. She wasn't afraid of anything.'

The year I was born, Nanima says, the talk of war grew loud. It was about water this time, both countries squabbling over the salty creeks and dry streambeds that lace the Rann of Kutch. Toxic nationalism grew. So did a movement for peace.

'Ten thousand people marched on both sides of the border. Gita and Amod marched too.'

'What happened?' I whisper.

'Tear gas. Lathis. They kept on, day after day. Then came the helicopters, the border police, the guns!'

Police. Guns. The words slams into me.

'They both died. My beautiful daughter and her husband.' She picks the pot up in her two hands and lifts it.

'They want to build a cleanup site,' I blurt out. 'Here. Alibhai Kaka told me.'

The pot slips from her hands, crashes on the floor. Grass seeds scatter. Nanima lets out a cry of anguish. The pot lies cracked in pieces; its reddish inside gleams.

We spend an hour picking up seeds and shards. 'Forgive me,' she says, over and over. 'This is yours. I meant to save it for you.'

'Nanima, what does it matter?'

She sighs. 'It's a beautiful world, potri. Sometimes, I think we people are its sickness.'

I see suddenly how thin she is and how she is starting to stoop.

Morning climbs toward the heat of noon and drags beyond it to a terrible stillness.

We talk until my throat is dry. We talk out life's hardness and the beauty of this salty land that is so easy to miss until you let yourself look closely. We talk about time stretching back into history, and all the people who have gone before us. We talk until we have talked and cried ourselves empty.

Nanima makes chai. We sit on a mat outside the house, sipping.

Patchy clouds are blowing in when a familiar bellow demands attention. Rani is bringing the herd back home.

The buffaloes crowd in through the compound gate. As I close it behind them, I hear a loud squawking carried on the breeze. Now the day folds in a new direction, life holding onto life.

As dusty haze turns to raindrops, I see something on the horizon. Nanima gasps, rises to her feet. It's a flock of flamingoes! They haven't come in years. They circle, come in for a landing. Will they nest in the low islands that dot the wide salt inlets? Will they lay eggs? Is this even possible? Perhaps there will be stick-legged chicks.

The minute they hatch, Nanima says, those chicks will start walking towards the water.

Uma Krishnaswami was born in India and is the author of many books for young readers. Her children's novel, Step Up to the Plate Maria Singh, won the Asian Pacific American Literature Award. Uma lives in Victoria, British Columbia, Canada. She has recently become a grandmother.

Saathi

Shazaf Haider

Our story begins in a divided land near an isolated hamlet: a place of cool streams and snow-kissed mountains and green, verdant valleys. The highest peak that stood guard over this small village rose to the sky like an unsheathed sword. On its base snaked a narrow strip of land, flanked on both sides by Y-shaped posts holding up coils upon coils of barbed wire.

To one side, the Pakistanis manned their posts. On the other, the Indians stood alert, ready to fire if given the command. In Kashmir, along the line of control, silence was coated with blood.

On both sides of this barren no man's land stood almost identical observation towers: tall, lonely rises of criss-crossed iron covered by corrugated tin, kept in place by bricks. The strip of no man's land was the narrowest here, so the sepoys atop these towers stood no further than thirty yards from each other.

Patrolling the towers was as dangerous as it was tedious: when violence broke out, the sepoys manning them were usually the first casualties of a cessation of ceasefire. The rest of the battalion was stationed a good mile away, under covered bunkers where the living quarters and food and armoury were situated.

On top of one tower stood Irshad Basheer, carrying a G3 rifle. A tall, slim, clean-shaven young man in his early twenties, he had joined the army after losing family and friends in an Indo-Pak war. He had vowed to avenge his country by joining the army and fighting the good fight.

On the other tower, in a bullet-proof vest and also heavily armed, patrolled Ramandeep Singh. Big-bellied and long-bearded, he had a loud laugh and merry, blue eyes. But his sunny disposition clouded over every time he remembered the day he became an orphan. Ramandeep had been ten when his father, soaking the sun on his charpoy in the village near the Indian post, had been killed by enemy shelling. He had waited for the day he was old enough to enlist: he would avenge his father and defend his country against the bastards who had ended his childhood with one violent attack.

Both men were ready for war.

But most of the time, war didn't come. Instead, there was the silence of the mountains and the indifference of the grey sky and the emptiness of a rocky outpost where nothing exciting happened. The only interesting thing that Irshad and Ramandeep ever saw was each other. After weeks upon endless weeks atop those towers, the fire of war that flickered in their breasts was eventually dampened by all-encompassing, mind-numbing, shin-tingling boredom.

Tedium gave way to discomfort one cold night in the winter rain. Irshad and Ramandeep had the night shift and both struggled to keep awake. Sleep weighed heavily on Irshad and he knew he needed to do something to last for four more hours until the end of his shift. He was miserable and cold and his eyes kept closing—there was no way he would be able to stay awake for four more hours until the end of his shift. He raised his eyes and saw Ramandeep huddled on his post, across the misty haze. Tired of sitting still, Irshad got up and stretched and leaned against the sandbags that lined the railing. Raising his voice, he called out: 'Haan bhai, Saathi, is all well with you?'

Ramandeep was startled from the stupor that had descended on him. He reached for the rifle and kept quiet. But the rain kept falling and the darkness engulfed them and Irshad's greeting offered a temporary respite from the all-pervasive loneliness of his duty. He got up and raised a hand. 'All is well here, saathi. How about with you?'

'Allahu Akbar. Things are peaceful.'

'Waheguru. Here too.'

'Have a good night.'

'Needs to stop raining for that to happen, saathi.'

Irshad chuckled in response and both men, now awake, went back to their posts and counted the minutes till they were relieved from their watch.

The next evening was cloudy but dry and Ramandeep and Irshad sniffed and sneezed as they manned their posts. Ramandeep's sneezes made Irshad chuckle, because they sounded like a little girl falling down an open sewer. Irshad's explosions, however, sounded like a bullet ricocheting off a cement pavement.

'Are there Kalashnikovs going off on your side, saathi?' Ramandeep asked mischievously just as Irshad tipped his head back for a sneeze.

'No, friend. Only in my head. This is a nasty cold.'

'That it is, saathi.'

'I bet I can sneeze more than you by nightfall.' Ramandeep said.

Irshad let rip another loud 'Aachoo'.

Each felt a certain camaraderie in their shared ailment. By midnight, he was five sneezes ahead—he called across to Ramandeep and told him the score. 'I'm winning,' he declared to the darkness.

'You get to win this one, Kalashnikov. But when India and Pakistan play the next match, it will be my turn to beat you.'

'Don't count on it: we defeated you in the last test match, saathi.'

'True, you did, but only after Tendulkar caught out your last batsman.'

'That catch was a beauty. Even I need to say so.'

'Thank you, saathi.'

'Almost as good as the one Akram took to get rid of Jadeja a few years ago.'

'The one-handed one? I thought it was going for a boundary when your man appeared out of nowhere.'

'Yes. It was a miracle.'

'True. That was a good one, I have to admit.'

A silence ensued. Ramandeep's effeminate sneeze interrupted the quiet and Irshad chuckled loudly. 'You're still four behind.'

'Oi don't you worry, I'll catch up by dawn.'

During the day, the two avoided conversation as there were enough ears awake and listening. But every couple of hours, Irshad raised his hand to enquire if all was well, and Ramandeep nodded and put his hand on his chest as if to say, 'Yes, thank you for asking.'

One sunny morning, an eagle soared high above with a snake in its beak. Irshad gesticulated towards Ramandeep, who clutched his rifle and leaned against the railing and looked to where his friend was pointing. Both men stared in wonder at the snake flailing in the air in the talons of a mighty eagle, which seemed impervious to the muscular writhing of its prey. As the bird disappeared in the sky, both men were aware of the other as a constant companion and a joint witness to this savage place.

As the weeks passed into months, Irshad and Ramandeep began to communicate in bits during the later afternoons when their commanding officers were asleep inside the bunkers. Opportunities for fun were availed: once, during the daily post-inspection, Irshad's post commander was exchanging some words with him. Ramandeep saw Irshad standing to attention and began to sneeze, knowing that Irshad found the sound hilarious. Each sneeze made Irshad suppress an unprofessional chuckle. His post commander was a humourless man who would not understand or appreciate the joke, so he dug his nails in his hands to avoid laughing at each 'Acheeeenk' across the border. Once the inspection was completed and the colonel gone, Irshad turned to Ramandeep and waved a fist at him, shaking his head and chuckling as his friend puts his hand on his knees and guffawed.

The days continued to pass and both sides' vigilance descended into a bored relaxation. In the bunkers, situated a good distance from the towers, officers played cards and ludo and sometimes listened to the radio. The day was broken up by meal times, which were an unappetizing affair since tinned food was the only fare at bay. The smells of daal and masala vegetables wafted across the no man's land, undetected by motion sensors. But unbeknown to Pakistani soldiers, a small crisis was brewing on the Indian side, where, by some unlucky happenstance, they found that they were fast running out of butter.

Ramandeep was a simple man of few needs, but one of the things he lived for was hot roti with butter and sugar for his morning breakfast. It gave a delicious start to an otherwise bland day. But the batallion cook reported that rations were low and soon, he would have to do with dry toast until the next batch of provisions arrived, which would not be for another month at least.

Sometimes it's the smallest things that threaten to undo the hardest of men. The prospect of doing without butter made Ramandeep abandon caution. That day, at sundown, he wrote a message on a torn piece of newspaper and tied it to a rock with a blue rubber band. There was enough light for Irshad to see Ramandeep on the other side waving something at him. Ramandeep put a finger on his lips and held up the stone, making an arc in the air, like a bowler towards a batsman.

Irshad understood. He looked down at his camp—the soliders were busy with maghrib prayers. He walked to the edge of the tower and leaned forward, cupping his hands like a wicketkeeper. Ramandeep tossed the rock across no man's land and it landed in Irshad's palms. Irshad pulled the rubber band off and opened the paper, on which was written: 'Saathi, do you have butter to spare? We are running out.' Irshad smiled, looked up at Ramandeep, and put his hand up as if to say, 'Let me arrange something.'

They were only thirty yards away, yet contact was almost impossible, as was an exchange of goods. When Irshad descended into his bunker after his shift at dawn, he spoke to the battalion cook who confirmed that they did, in fact, have plenty of butter in stock.

But how to arrange to send it to the other side? Colonel Ikram would not allow it or have much sympathy for the Indians' plight.

However, fate intervened when an Indian bakri squeezed itself between the coils onto the Pakistani side. The distressed Indian shepherd, its hapless owner, appealed to the Indian commander to allow him to retrieve it. A white flag was waved and Colonel Ikram and Lieutenant Commander Rao met below to discuss the possibility of allowing the shepherd to come get his goat. All eyes were focused on them, so no one saw another rock being tossed from Pakistan to India. On it was written, 'The Butter will be with the Bakri, saathi.'

That evening, Irshad requested a meeting with the Colonel and explained the situation to him. Colonel Ikram had a good laugh and thought it a good opportunity to bestow largesse upon the Indians and to shame them for their scarce supplies. Four tins of butter were tied to the belly of the goat as it was returned to the shepherd. Commander Rao received these with mixed feelings—he didn't want to be indebted to the enemy, but he knew that dwindling rations were causing discontent among the sepoys, and morale in these abandoned and remote places was always in a precarious state. So he made a great show of inspecting the tins and declared he would accept the 'offering of peace' from the enemy. Later, he told his soldiers that Pakistan was intimidated by the impressive Indian military presence and wanted to appease them in case they went to war.

The next morning, Ramandeep ate butter roti and said a small prayer for Irshad and his family.

The exchange of butter and bakri had the effect of lightening up everyone's mood. Pakistani and Hindi songs could be heard a little louder on both sides, and calls of 'Sab theek hai saathi?'

'Kaisay ho saathi' could be heard by other sepoys across the coils of wire.

But all this changed in a matter of days. The Indians report a terrorist infiltration in the glaciers and shoot at the Pakistan army. The Indian prime minister allows this skirmish to gain more traction than it would otherwise have gotten because elections are coming up and conflict is a good way to garner votes and support. The Pakistani army tells the government that it will retaliate and it does, from the plains to the mountains.

Conflict snakes its way up the line of control. Some miles south of the hamlet, an Indian military van is fired at. Ramandeep is given the order to stand alert and shoot if there is any provocation from the Pakistani side. He looks at Irshad, who has also been given the same order.

Extra sandbags were hauled up to them for protection against stray bullets. They crouched behind them, staring at each other. Even now, it was quiet, but tense. Many times, Irshad wanted to call out to Ramandeep, but hesitated. This was not the time for friendship.

A rat scuttled across the no man's land and triggered a landmine. The sound of the blast was followed by calls of 'Allah-u-Akbar' and 'Jai Hind.' Guns went off and bullets were fired and grenades were tossed. On his tower, Ramandeep closed his eyes and begged for forgiveness as he shot at Irshad, ducking when he, too, was fired at. This continued for a while until he noticed that no more bullets were coming his way. He raised his head cautiously and then stood up, staring in horror at the blood-coated sandbags on the opposite tower. Irshad was flung lifelessly upon them.

They had called each other 'saathi' even though they were enemies. Together, they had stood on their solitary towers, holding their guns and wiping their noses. They had become the unlikeliest of friends. They had been forced to shoot at each other. One saathi had died at the hands of the other.

He retreated behind his fortification and wept hot tears of grief and regret. And then he picked up the gun and continued to shoot at the soldiers scurrying below, because that is what he was meant to do.

The violence came in waves of deafening sound and descents of eerie quiet. Ramandeep managed to descend from his tower and take shelter in the bunker. The shelling continued for days until a ceasefire was announced and white flags were waved on both sides to indicate that they were ready to observe it. Both sides claimed victory—both sides declared that the enemy had been taught a lesson. And in a matter of a month, some semblance of normalcy had returned.

Ramandeep once again resumes his post on the observation tower. Another jawaan with a fierce moustache and angry eyes glowers back at him. His stance is aggressive and his rifle pointed straight at Ramandeep, who mirrors his show of hostility. They resume watch but there is no interaction and no friendship. Every day, Ramandeep eats dry toast and prays for his saathi to be received by the angels in heaven.

Irshad's name and picture were printed in the local papers and he was given a medal of valour and his uniform was delivered to his grieving mother, wrapped in his country's flag.

Our story ends with one saathi being lowered into the ground near his hometown of Multan, while the other continues his watch on the observation tower, the note reading 'The Butter will be with the Goat, saathi' folded neatly in his breast pocket. Their brief and unlikely friendship ended while the war continued.

Shazaf Fatima Haider is the author of *How It Happened* and *A Firefly in the Dark*. She is currently working on her third novel. She lives with her husband and four children in St Albans.

'A Spy! A Spy!'

Farrukh Nadeem

The panic had not spread that far yet, but the people decided to migrate. Leaving their homes behind and moving away with their cattle was not easy at all. Many were now spending more time with the retired schoolmaster, Hameed, the only '*noble*' man in the village. The thumping of the tanks moving around the border areas would wreak havoc on the nerves of the residents and they would turn to Master Hameed's Haveli.

One evening, one of the villagers drew near to the schoolmaster and said, 'Masterji, I have heard that the government has banned hunting.'

'Indeed,' said another, giving voice to the villagers' thoughts, 'some officials even went to Lala's big mansion. They told him that firing for the purpose of hunting can be risky in these circumstances. "The Sikh soldiers are already on the border," they said, "How are they to know if it's one of us shooting a deer or if it's the soldiers?"'

'So, what did Lala say?' Masterji asked as he turned to look at the villager, taking a puff from his hookah as he spoke.

'I... I could not listen,' he stammered, shifting uncomfortably at the question. 'I was too busy moving about, serving food, etc.'

'I have also heard,' said another, staring directly at the schoolmaster 'that they have appointed Lala as protector, as guardian and leader in these troubled times.'

'Ah, but Lala owns us, you see!' Master Hameed stared at his audience. 'He owns everything! He owns the land, the water, the masjid. He even owns our baithak! We have no control over things, no say in war, no say in peace. We are nothing! Just some villagers, farmers, travellers in this life! Our fates are in Lala's hands, and in the hands of the One above...'

'And why would Lala care?' a depressed villager asked. 'He fed splendid food to the guests, even opened a few bottles. And these big shots...they forget everything over drinks! Lala laughed out loud, telling his guests that he would talk to the villagers, but also said that "*all's fair in love and war.*"'

'And then what happened?' a villager asked, drawing closer to his friend.

'What do you think happened? They ate, drank, and went their own ways! The driver unlocked the Pajero, and Lala... well, he wore his suit and got in with his guards and then off they went, towards the city.'

A few days passed. Masterji's visitors had decreased in number. In the evening, shopkeepers who had set up shop outside the village and the few men who had acquired government jobs would cycle back to their homes. On their way, they would be stopped by curious gossipers who would ask for the latest headlines. Having thus acquired a quick rundown of the newspapers, the villagers could feel the tensions rising as the sounds of war knocked slowly on the fragile doors of peace. Particularly concerning were the speeches given by A.B.Vajpayee and his supporters. Panting excitedly, the men would then rush to Masterji's house, where they would unload their thoughts and opinions over hookah and some sweets.

The schoolmaster, seeing emotions rise like the bubbling of a hookah, had once remarked that difficult times are a man's test. 'Have you not seen,' he said, 'that birds and animals huddle together in a storm? In these moments of confusion, anything is possible. One small mistake, the tiniest bit of mischief, the smallest spark can become the flame that can burn our lives, and our peace, to the ground.'

It was around this time that the masjids made an announcement. Everywhere, in all of the border villages, the same message repeated itself again and again. 'These are uncertain times. The enemy could strike us at any moment. He is willing to do anything, and his spies may have already infiltrated our ranks. Beware of strangers! Watch them carefully. Protect our weaknesses in this time of strife.' The Maulvi Sahib of Nurkot said something similar. His head covered by his turban, his chest swollen, he roared into the microphone. 'Gentlemen,' he said, 'the unbeliever is treacherous. He is a niggard with a devilish mind who wants to attack us once again in the dark night. The Islamic world is surrounded by enemies, we have a thousand foes all around, but who can stand in front of our faith? Victory is our fate, defeat is theirs. Our brave soldiers stand between us! If you see a spy, teach him a lesson that he never forgets! Vajpayee, if you can hear me, listen! Try whatever mischief you want to—we will quash it like we will quash you!'

This, of course, was no call to war, but its effect was no less potent. The possibility of danger, of being attacked from within, created even more unrest. The serpent had entered the garden and the poison of doubt was running in the very veins of the land. Some people started packing. Others wondered about their relatives. Yet others stared blankly at the cracked walls of their homes. There were no telephones. The announcements had been made, which meant there was not enough time to write letters. One side of the village was landlocked and there was no danger. Or not yet, at least...on the other side, empty land, but land where rainwater had collected and the landowners were now growing rice. Leaving immediately could be disastrous! The people stared at each other, hoping to find consolation. What else could be done?

Untouched by all this were the four villagers who sat in Lala's mansion. These four were known locally as the hunters and were busy even now, sharing the exploits of their hunting dogs. They were proudly narrating the adventures of their dogs—sometimes their teeth snapping in the air or ruthlessly grabbing the neck of a cat, a rabbit, or a ringed turtle-dove. Their sense of smell was impeccable and was praised endlessly by their owners.

Afternoons were extremely hot, and so the four would resort to the coolest part of the building. Back there, they had a number of rooms for tying up the animals. To the right, there was a small room for tractor tires, engine parts, diesel, spare wiring, spades, pickaxes, and a bunch of other tools. Right beside it was a cabin divided into two parts; one, in which the four now sat, and the other that now housed some broken ploughs, a yoke, an old sword that once belonged to Lala's grandfather (the 'Elder Lala') and had tasted much blood in 1947, some sickles, and an old wooden frame that was once used to draw water from the well. It was also said that the cabin was haunted, that it was frequented by jinns and demons. Many servants, in fact, had heard strange voices, male and female, coming from this cabin. Under the dim light of an old yellow bulb, one of the hunters expressed anger at the old fan and its cooling. Taking off his dirty shirt, he hung it on the wall and then turned to his friends.

'Yaar, it is too hot in here! Let's go to the river and swim?'

His friend, Makha, laughed at this and said, 'Seriously, Jin Watta? Even the heat would run away from you! With a body of stone, do you still feel hot?'

At this, their third friend Rangu placed his right hand under his armpit and produced strange sounds by waving his left elbow. He smiled mockingly at Jin Watta, making fun of him. He was blind in one eye and was considered the village jester. He would often make others laugh with these armpit sounds, his elbow moving up and down like an old-fashioned water pump. He was even proud of being Lala's lackey.

Makha had once served as a caretaker of Lala's Lahore mansion, which his family had been looking after since 1980. He now worked as a tractor driver and was excited about his promotion.

The fourth and final member of this gang was known as Jeru Kedu. He had lost a leg by accidentally triggering a landmine. He had been sneaking across the border to hunt, and even though he had lost his leg, he never lost his passion for hunting. His father and grandfather had been Lala's accountants while their ancestors had been loyal servants even before the Partition. Ten years ago, Rangu's father had been killed in a feud involving Lala's family. Since then, Rangu, without caring for himself or his well-being, had devoted himself to Lala's service. The villagers said that he could do anything for Lala, and that he would carry out all orders, good or bad, without hesitation and in all probability, ruthlessly and with pleasure.

The four hunters were famous in all the surrounding villages for their friendship and loyalty towards Lala. After work, the four of them would spend time hunting or playing cards. And whenever Lala wished to hunt, these four were his companions. They were such skilled hunters, well-trained by their Lala, that they could smell the prey even before the hunting dogs. Two of the four, in fact, were even said to be among Lala's close confidants. When the hunting trip would end, the four would place the prey in the Pajero and drive it back to the mansion without leaving behind any hints. Inside, they would retreat to their cabin and recall their exploits from the trip, all of them laying claim to the greatest kill, like four jackals sinking their teeth into a young deer and then arguing over the division. Their dogs too would participate in this. They would bark, growl, and then snap at the spoils, pulling at dead skin to throw at their feet.

Today, like any other day, they were sitting in the same cabin. Suddenly, some noise was heard in the street.

Jinn Watta glanced about the room, surprised. 'Oi, Rangu,' he said, 'see what's going on.'

The noise, meanwhile, had gotten louder, so they flung themselves, all four of them, to the window. Outside, some young boys from the village had formed a mob. Fleeing from them was a lone figure, a young nomad girl who made and sold wooden horses (*gug-gu ghorey*). They were following her and screaming, 'A Spy! A Spy!'

Makha winked at Rangu and said, 'Hey, go see what's happening.'

As soon as he opened the gates, Rangu placed his hand under his armpit and proceeded to make the same sounds. The mob immediately stopped shouting and the street was filled with the boys' laughter.

The post-monsoon humid weather and its heat had, by now, filled the air with sweat and stench, and this multiplied the vulnerability of the nomad girl. The devilish serpent snapped again, making doubt and suspicion hang in people's breaths. Onlookers and whisperers could be seen, loitering around the street corners.

What was going on? The nomad girl glanced around her in panic. With the cloth sack of wooden toys resting on her head, she looked here and there, like a dove caught in a hunter's trap. She gazed at the people around her, as if asking them one question. 'Spy?' When she realized that she was being labelled as an 'Indian spy' she trembled with fear. She pleaded and swore on her innocence; she even opened her little sack! But in return, she received the same sounds from Rangu's armpit and bellowing howls of laughter. Rangu turned around and looked at his friends, who signalled a message.

'Hurry up, will you, you're establishing a court out there!'

He understood. With his one eye, he watched the nomad girl wipe the sweat off her face. He smelled fresh sweat. He said, 'We must search her, she might have hidden a wireless somewhere!' Then, turning to the people, he said 'Wait here, we will search her, and then we'll decide... If she's a spy... well, the police station is not far.'

On the mention of *police*, the nomad girl assented to being searched. She didn't realize what was happening. With her sack on her head, she vanished into the labyrinth of the mansion. Seeking her hidden 'wireless', eight different hands started dancing over her, like small spiders scuttling on a dark floor. Outside, one could still hear the echoing cries, 'A Spy! A Spy!' She was taken to the old cabin, where the old lightbulb still fought the dark. She was told to sit in the pile of old junk, where the sack that had rested so firmly on her head was removed. The shirts had already disappeared. An unseen signal turned off the light. In the dark, the nomad girl could not even tell how many men were around her. She stared, terrified, at the dark, mumbling and pleading to be freed.

All of a sudden, a *Lali*, a common mynah, panicking and screaming, broke into the din of the hunt. It had been trapped in when they had hastily closed the doors. When the lights were turned off, she panicked and began fluttering and crashing about, screaming and wailing of her captivity. Jeru stumbled for a bit, his eyes red with rage.

'Rangu,' he growled, 'twist her neck, will you... shut her up!'

Rangu let the door open slightly and then chased the bird around, making the same noises from under his armpit to scare the bird away. The mynah glanced one last time at the nomad girl and flew out of the door, screaming loudly.

In the little light that had snuck into the room, the nomad girl looked around her. She saw three—no, four!—faces, all of them alike, and behind them she saw, hanging from the cabin roof, many long and hideous tongues that were slowly reaching out. It seemed as if spit were dripping down from the ceiling, with a smell so strong and hideous that the cabin itself would have shaken. Jinn Watta picked up the old sword, and pointing it to her neck, he spoke.

'We will cut you into a million pieces. Just do as I say!'

But why be silent? That little bird had left her with an important message. Three pairs of hands pulled at her, but she would not move. She lay face down on the floor, refusing to obey. Her mouth let out a perpetual scream. Outside, Rangu assured the people that it was nothing more than a search. If the people would grow weary, he would make the same sounds from his armpit to amuse them. Rangu heard a whistle from inside. He knew at once that the 'search' was almost over. It would now be his turn. Rushing inside, he entered the cabin with a question.

'Has the problem been solved?'

'Solved? Nothing is solved! How could it be solved when she doesn't shut up?' Jinn Watta looked furious. 'Go,' he said, 'talk to her! Tell her to pipe down! Tell her to stop resisting! Or else... Or else she'll lose her life! I swear... I swear I will wring her neck!'

Closing the door shut, Rangu made his way to the back. Looking at his victim, he spoke, 'Oh, look at this! She is lying all straight! I will give her a calf from the herd, only if she quiets down...'

The nomad girl was lying still on her stomach. Her eyes closed, she had done her best to stay untouched. The first three had pulled at her, torn her clothes, broken her bangles till they hurt her arms. This fourth person's words pierced her, like the broken bangles into a broken heart. Lying with her face to the floor, she could feel the blood seeping into her nostrils. For a minute, she felt that the village huts would no longer wait for her return. Her eyes watered, as if the bangles they had broken had now melted and flown like grief from her eyes. Jeru Kedu, like Rangu before him, was trying to convince the crowd. He held a bamboo under his arm, speaking with authority.

'Do not worry, she will speak! She'll even tell us the names of their dogs! Will not be able to pretend for long, she will tell us everything!'

First Rangu and now Jeru... The women, and even the men, were going back to their work. It was probably all an act, an elaborate fraud! Some of the boys, bent on mischief, stayed on to chat with Jeru, making jokes with obvious double-meanings about the interrogation. After some time, the sensible lot started to leave, saying 'Is she even a spy?' The nomad girl spread her hand outwards to adjust her tattered headcloth. She felt something sharp. It was a sickle, with sharp teeth and an edge! Quickly, she hid it under her body while holding it with her right hand. Rangu, foolishly, had taken her frightful silence to be consent. Rubbing one hand on his stomach, he leapt down towards the floor, only to be met by a sharp pain that went all the way out through his back. A painful scream echoed out from the cabin, reaching the nearby streets.

The three hunters burst into the room. Turning on the light, they first leapt in the direction of the scream. A moment later, they turned back; jumping over what remained of Rangu, they turned off the lightbulb and rushed to the outer gate, like prey fleeing for its life.

For a minute, silence pervaded the air.

Those who were startled by the screams, and those who had left, were now returning. The hunters could not have imagined that Rangu would fall, face-first, onto a sickle. They had barely managed to say his name—'Rangu'—when the nomad girl, wrapped in her tattered clothes, her cloth sack resting on her head, came out. Wide-eyed, Jeru Kedu, Makha, and Jinn Watta stared at the street and then at the nomad girl. Her clothes were obviously stained with blood. What should they do? What could they say? Nothing made sense for a moment. Then, stumbling about on his one foot, Jeru Kedu burst out in a quivering voice.

'Spy! A Spy!'

The men and women of the village saw the cloth sack ripping open and the wooden toys falling from the girl's head. Lala and the crowd in the street were seen making the same strange sounds with their armpits.

'A Spy! A Spy! A Spy! A Spy!'

Translated from the Urdu by Muhammad Munhib Shah and Abdal Ahmed Jafri

---

Farrukh Nadeem is lecturer in English at International Islamic University Islamabad. He is the author of *Fiction, Discourse and Cultural Spatiality in Urdu*. That book is considered to be an admirable contribution to the ongoing discussions in contemporary literary criticism. Farrukh's short stories have also been published in various literary magazines on both sides of the border, Pakistan and India.

Un-Sistered

Shahbano Bilgrami

It all happened so suddenly, thought Laila. It was late March, and the heavy storm clouds above their small town in Upstate New York promised rain. The world outside Laila's window seemed worn and dreary, still suspended in mid-winter when it should have been turning green, bursting with life, warming her fingers as she traced patterns on the frosted glass. Pulling on her sweater, she walked over to the bulletin board above her desk and scanned the photographs and cards that she had pinned to it over the year. There was that selfie she took when the family went to Keuka Lake last summer, the ribbon she won at the Geography Bee, some silly doodles from her seventh-grade sketch book, even an old recipe of her Nani's written in blue ink. She paused at the picture on the top-left of her last birthday party. There she was, surrounded by her friends in the glow of the thirteen candles on her birthday cake. Monica and Louise, Tammy, Raina, Chantal—they were all there, and so was she, Maahi, the girl who had once been her closest friend.

Laila first met Maahi when they were four. They went to the same Montessori school at the edge of Winters Road, a small low building with a metal sun above the entrance, its rays curling at the ends like Maahi's hair. As soon as they met, they were inseparable, doing classwork together and playing knee-deep in the moist sandbox, preparing lopsided cakes that dried and cracked in the sun. The teachers would often confuse them with one another, they were so alike, dark hair and eyes, tanned skin the colour of caramel, running around the playground with their plaits flying in the air. Laila and Maahi, Maahi and Laila. Their mothers would sit on a nearby bench at pick-up time and smile as the girls, wearing bright sweaters and hats with bows or pointy cat's ears, would huddle inside the old sailboat that lay moored in the grass. Fairies or sprites, fantastical creatures or superheroes, the girls found a way of keeping themselves busy. No one could imagine Laila and Maahi apart. They were always one of a pair.

'Zehra, these goras think that all of us desis look the same, just like we think all goras look the same!' Aditi laughed as she showed Laila's mother the letter she received from the school accountant. 'See, it's addressed to your family, and he handed it to me! Can you believe that?'

Laughing, Laila's mom agreed. 'That's so true. Sometimes I think Mrs Randall can't tell Laila and Maahi apart. Be careful, girls!' she added as they rolled down the grassy rise and landed, giggling, in a dusty heap at their mothers' feet.

Out of all the games that they used to play, they loved 'ship-ship-sail.' Climbing into the old sailboat under the trees, Laila and Maahi would pretend they were journeying to different parts of the world. Sometimes it was India, sometimes Pakistan, sometimes it was far-off China to see the Great Wall or to South Africa for a jungle safari. More often than not, though, the countries that they sailed to in their imaginations were ones that were created out of air, whose borders were nebulous like suspended drops of rainwater, and whose rulers were peace-loving and kind and who welcomed Laila and Maahi like old friends. It was in these imaginary countries that they had the most fun, speaking to each other in their own made-up languages as they marveled at the amazing things they saw – hats seven feet high, trees that grew candies, houses made of silvery fish.

Laila and Maahi were more than friends, they were sisters. Sometimes their neighbors would mistake them for twins. In their small, remote town, far from the crowds of New York City, there were only a handful of South Asian families. Laila's father was a physician at the local hospital while Maahi's parents ran the main hotel on Market Street. In the early days, before other Muslim families arrived in the area, the Ahmeds celebrated Eid with their Indian friends and neighbours. On Diwali, the Sharmas would drive to New Jersey to return laden with sweets for Laila and her family. Both girls would wear brightly-coloured shalwar-kameezes or lehngas trimmed with silver and gold, bangles that shimmered on their chubby wrists, and elaborate henna on their palms as they swung high into the blue sky on Laila's backyard swings.

'I have no idea where the years have gone!' Zehra whispered to Aditi on the day of the girls' eighth grade graduation. Laila and Maahi stood on the stage in their prettiest dresses, their hair curled professionally at the salon in the mall, the excitement of the moment reflected in their dark eyes and smiling faces. Afterwards, when their parents were busy socializing, they joined their friends for ice-cream.

'Laila, Shal, come here,' called out Raina near the dessert table. 'Can you guys answer a question for us. Rita says that you're from India. I can't remember if that's what you told me, Laila...?'

'I'm from Pakistan,' Laila replied. 'Why do you ask anyway?'

'Well, we were just saying how it's always the Indian kids who win the spelling bees,' said Rita. 'I guess Indians are smarter than the rest of us!'

'I'm not sure about that,' Maahi grinned. 'I'm the worst speller around. I can barely even spell my own name!'

Although everyone laughed, to Laila, it felt strange to be talking about nationalities. After all, Laila and Maahi were as American as their friends. They were both born at the local hospital and had birth certificates to prove it. The only time it became relevant was once a year, on Cultural Day, when their mothers set up tables for each country and prepared snacks for the school community. The reality was that in their day-to-day existence they both had so many things in common. One day, when their parents sat them down and showed them a map of the subcontinent, Maahi's father traced his family's migration from Sahiwal in Pakistan to Ludhiana in India. 'And, do you know,' Laila's father Javaid exclaimed excitedly, 'this is where my family once lived, here in Delhi which is the capital of India? During the Partition, our family went in the opposite direction and eventually settled in Karachi, Pakistan.'

Laila and Maahi never really worried about these things, though. They were American. More than that, they were best friends. Their friendship didn't depend on what they ate or where their grandparents once lived.

Or so they had thought.

Laila found it difficult to believe that one day, in all of those years of friendship, could change everything, but it had. She wished she could forget it all, but it played out against the white of her bedroom walls each morning like a cinema reel. It was a bad dream that she couldn't shake off no matter how hard she tried.

The sequence was always the same: it had been her parents' anniversary in mid-October, there was to be a huge party arranged by Maahi's mother later that day. After breakfast, Laila had gone to Maahi's house where they had made cards and handmade gifts for the party, wrapping them up in gold paper and silver ribbon. At five, Maahi's mother had called up to them, 'we'll be leaving for Thali at six, girls. Please be ready. We can't be late!'

Laila remembered the scramble to get dressed, the zips and buttons hastily done, the shoes pulled on, hair brushed in a hurry, even lipstick tried on for the very first time. How grown up they had felt as they entered the restaurant that evening in their fancy new dresses! Joining the guests in the party room, they waited in excitement. Then, there were urgent calls for quiet, the lights were dimmed, one, two, three...

'Surprise!' everyone had yelled as Laila's parents walked in to shouts and laughter.

'Aditi, when did you arrange all of this?' Zehra had asked as she looked around the room at the dozens of well-wishers who had gathered to celebrate. 'It's so true what they say—in America, friends are family!' Laughing, she had hugged Maahi's mother while their fathers shook hands and patted each other on the back.

It would have been the perfect evening, if the adults hadn't ruined it. It had all started with a random comment carelessly tossed into the air above the dimly lit table where they sat. To this day, Laila didn't know who had said it. Sometimes, as she thought over the events of that evening, it seemed her father had, at other times, Maahi's dad. It could have been anyone at that table. It didn't matter in the end who had started it because within minutes, chairs were pushed back, people were standing. Words, hard and shiny, were pitted against each other. 'Javaid, Tarun, please—let's not discuss politics!' their mothers had pleaded. 'It never leads to anything good. Haven't we spent enough time here to help heal those old wounds between our countries?' Laila felt Maahi's hand reach out to her hold hers under the table. The taste of spice burned Laila's tongue as she watched words—simple words—tear a decade of friendship apart.

'Mama,' Laila had later asked in tears, 'why do Maahi and I have to end our friendship because our dads had a fight?' Her mother just shook her head and hugged her close, telling her that one day they would all be friends again. But, as time wore on, that seemed more and more unlikely. The families stopped meeting, there were no more telephone conversations, no more girls' trips to the mall or to the park.

Laila removed the birthday photograph from the bulletin board and wished she could go back in time. It had been almost six months since she had last spoken to Maahi. No, Maahi hadn't moved to a distant city or another state. In fact, she still lived only three blocks away in the very same house she had grown up in. Laila remembered every inch of that house, from the cracked stone steps that led to the front door to the sloping raftered ceilings of their lounge to the wide window above Maahi's desk from which they used to spy on the boy who lived across the street. Laila was sure Maahi still remembered the Ahmed house as if it were her own. After all, they were practically sisters.

Laila didn't think it was possible to 'un-sister' someone whom you had grown up with, and wondered if Maahi felt that too. Now that they had started high school, they had no classes together and only saw each other briefly in the halls or on the school bus. Laila missed her best friend and wished that they could go back to the days when their relationship was simple and uncomplicated, just two little girls playing dress up and baking cookies or climbing to the very top of the highest tree at the park. She couldn't just throw all of that away.

That day, Laila was quieter than usual on the school bus. She placed her backpack on the seat next to her so that no one would sit there until Maahi's stop. She knew she was taking a risk. It would be so embarrassing if Maahi ignored her invitation, but Laila was determined to try. Her palms sweaty and heart beating wildly, she watched as the bus slowly lumbered up the hill to Maahi's house. There she stood in her lavender jacket and blue jeans, her dark hair pulled back, her familiar school bag slung on her shoulder. Laila must have seen her standing like this at the bus stop over a thousand times since they were little girls. Her mind raced as she thought of all the ways she could persuade Maahi to give their friendship another chance.

Maahi climbed onto the bus and began walking towards the back. 'Now,' Laila thought, but before she could say anything, Maahi had already passed her and was waving to her other friends. Disappointed, Laila squeezed her eyes shut and wished that she had been quicker, more brave. Suddenly, she felt a hand on her shoulder.

'Is this seat taken?' It was Maahi.

'Yes, it is,' Laila replied with a nervous smile. 'Actually,' she continued haltingly, 'I was saving it for you.'

Maahi laughed as she sat down next to her, her hair catching the watery sunlight that was now streaming in through the trees. 'Laila, I've missed you so much!' she said, turning to hug her.

'I've missed you too, Maahi. After all, we're sisters.'

Shahbano Bilgrami is a published poet, novelist, and educational consultant with over two decades of experience writing and editing for children. Her publications for young readers include four-book adventure series *Munna Man and Baby Lady* (OUP Pakistan 2017) and the *Starlight Reading Programme* (Lightstone Publishers Ltd 2022). Her debut novel, *Without Dreams* (HarperCollins 2007), was longlisted for the Man Asian Literary Prize 2007, and her second book, *Those Children* (HarperCollins 2017), was long listed for the DSC Prize for South Asian Fiction 2017.

About the Translators

Rakhshanda Jalil

Rakhshanda Jalil is a multi-award-winning translator, writer, and literary historian. She has published over 25 books and written over 50 academic papers and essays. Some of her books include *Liking Progress, Loving Change: A Literary History of the Progressive Writers Movement in Urdu*, a biography of Urdu feminist writer *Dr Rashid Jahan: A Rebel and her Cause* and a translation of Intizar Hussain's *The Sea Lies Ahead*, among others.

Bina Biswas

Bina Biswas, a former professor of English Language, holds a PhD in English from Andhra University. She has authored thirteen books including 5 major translations and two poetry books.

Maaz Bin Bilal

Maaz Bin Bilal is a poet, translator, and academic. His first collection, *Ghazalnama: Poems from Delhi, Belfast, and Urdu*, was shortlisted for the Sahitya Akademi Yuva Puraskar. His translation of Fikr Taunsvi's Partition diary, *The Sixth River*, has been critically appreciated, and his translation of Ghalib's Banaras poem, Chirag-e-Dair, is forthcoming. Maaz teaches literary studies at Jindal Global University, India.

Priyanka Sarkar

Priyanka Sarkar is a translator, editor and writer. She has translated Chitra Mudgal's, *Giligadu* (Niyogi Books 2019) and Shivani's *Bhairavi* (Yoda Press-Simon & Schuster 2020) into English. Her translations of short stories from Hindi to English have been published by OUP, *Scroll.in*, *South Asian Review*, Audible and Women Unlimited. Her biography on Shakuntala Devi is available on Storytel.

Shad Naveed

Shad Naved teaches comparative literature at B.R. Ambedkar University, Delhi and translates from Urdu to Hindi, Arabic, Spanish and French. His recent translations include *The Hindi Canon: Intellectuals, Processes, Criticism* (Tulika Books) and *The Incomparable Festival* (Penguin Classics).

Harsh Pant

Coming from the hills of Uttarakhand, India, Harsh Pant believes in the 'write' side of the brain. She has around 40 aired radio stories to her credit along with an anthology of short stories.

Mandira Chakraborty

Mandira Chakraborty is a Researcher in Medical Humanities and Narrative Medicine who teaches English Literature at a College in Kolkata. She has dabbled in poetry, prose (the memoir format) in English, but this is her first translation work. She writes and thinks in English and reads a lot of Hindi nowadays.

Abdal Ahmed Jafri

Abdal Ahmed Jafri is a Lahore-based fiction writer, translator and film reviewer. He has written extensively in various publications on history, entertainment and sports. His book *Saadat Hassan aur Manto* was published by Nigarshat Publishers in 2013.

Muhammad Munhib Shah

Muḥammad Munhib Shah holds an MPhil degree in English Literature and teaches as a visiting lecturer at the International ʾIslāmic University, ʾIslāmābād, and the Quāʿid-i-Aʿzam University. He translates in his free time, writes poetry, and spends much time studying and teaching the traditional ʾIslāmic sciences, including, among others, the spiritual realm—Taṣawwuf.

About the Illustrator

Priya Kuriyan is a children's book writer-illustrator and comics maker and chronic doodler. She has directed educational films for the Sesame Street show (India) and the Children's Film Society of India (CFSI), and has illustrated numerous children's books. In 2019, she won the 'Big Little Book Award' instituted by Parag, an initiative of Tata Trusts to recognize her contribution to children's literature in India. She lives and works in the city of Bangalore and in her spare time makes funny caricatures of its residents.